THE
BENICA
BELLE

THE
BENICIA
BELLE

Larry Jay Martin

G·K·Hall&Co.

Boston, Massachusetts
1993

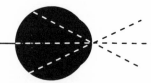

This Large Print Book carries the Seal of Approval of N.A.V.H.

Published in Large Print by arrangment with
Bantam Books, a division of
Bantam Doubleday Dell Publishing Group, Inc.

G.K. Hall Large Print Book series.

British Commonwealth Rights courtesy of
Bantam Books, a division of
Bantam Doubleday Dell Publishing Group, Inc.

Printed on acid free paper in the United States of America.

Set in 18 pt. Plantin.

Library of Congress Cataloging-in-Publication Data

Martin, Larry Jay.

    The Benicia belle / Larry Jay Martin.
        p. cm. — (G.K. Hall large print book series.)
    ISBN 0-8161-5609-3 (alk. paper)
    1. Large type books.   I. Title.
[PS3563.A72487B4   1993]
813'.54—dc20   92–32527

R.G. Miller
Harry Tibbet
and
R.M. "Bob" Pyles

for some blisters and knots on the
head, but also for many hours of great
gin, pitch, and cribbage and many years
of good advice

The rapid piercing cry of a victorious peregrine falcon cut the stillness. Clint lifted his eyes. Droplets flung from a water snake's tail as it writhed spasmodically in the bird's claws. A circle of ripples marked the spot in the quiet cattail-rimmed backwater where the raptor had snatched the snake, and the air reverberated with powerful wing beats as bird lifted flailing reptile up and over the tules.

Clint realized he had been dozing in the saddle as Diablo plodded along.

Heat hung oppressively in the low valley and shimmered in the distance as mock pools of water, but the cool respite of the cottonwood-and-sycamore-shaded hacienda of Rancho del Rio Ancho lay only a few miles ahead—if the mosquitoes did not gnaw him down to the bone before he got there. Clint slapped at a particularly rapacious one on the back of his sun-reddened neck and laughed under his breath as he remembered Gideon's advice when he had left him and the foothills and started down into the swampy valley floor.

"Don't worry," Gideon had said, "there's not a single mosquito along the Sacramento. They're all married with plenty of hungry young'uns."

He had left Gideon to guard the horse herd down on the Kaweah when word reached him that Don Carlos Vega wanted to see him.

He watched the falcon rise over a line of cottonwoods, then was distracted by approaching sounds, and the desire for the shade and cool drinks that awaited lay overshadowed by curiosity.

"Let's take a look," Clint said to Diablo. Long ago he had worried about speaking aloud to a horse—but then, Diablo was not just any horse. Clint spent so much time alone on California trails with the big palomino stallion that he treated him more like the friend he had proven to be than a simple means of transportation. Diablo responded to a shift of weight and the slightest touch of rein.

Clint had heard the boats' shrill voices,

each steam whistle as distinctive as a fish-wife's shriek as they berated each other with long blasts, long before he could see them or hear the pounding of their engines. He knew they fought against the current, racing for the prime spot at Sacramento's embarcadero. The river wars, as the press labeled their fierce competition, fascinated him.

He reined Diablo up off the *carreta* trail toward the river—Point Chapman, where he knew the narrows of Steamboat Slough joined the main stream of the Sacramento River. The slough cut better than ten miles off the trip between Sacramento City and San Francisco, and time and distance was money to the highly competitive operators. Though it was narrow, shallow, and serpentine, the S.B. Slough, as she was not so lovingly known, had fewer snags than the deeper main artery of the muddy Sacramento. S.B. stood for "steamboat" when ladies, preachers, or other tender ears were near, and "som 'bitch" when they were not, and she had earned her nickname well.

The big palomino stallion broached a sandpaper-oak thicket, shouldered his way down through a stand of river willow to the edge of a wide patch of sharp-leafed tules—

3

flushing a score of blackbirds, a pair of mallards, a sand-hill crane, and a graceful trio of stilts from the quiet water there—then paused, snorted, and sidestepped nervously when his hooves began to suck at the river mud. The shrill echo of the whistles seemed to hurt his ears.

In the distance, the majestic sternwheeler *River Ruler* overtook the smaller side-wheeler *Queen Anne.*

The *Ruler's* wake ran bank to bank, a great V behind the boat, inundating the tules and sending egrets, herons, and red- and yellow-winged blackbirds into a wing-flapping, raucous retreat on each side of the quarter-mile-wide river. Great twin black streams of smoke trailed her, marking her passing, while lesser craft ahead—a pair of heavily laden, current driven, flat-bottom scows—scuddled aside to yield the deepest cut in the mud-colored river. Not doing so would risk being cut in half. The thump-thump-thump cadence of the *Ruler's* single giant steam-driven piston, the singsong creak of her gears, pulleys, and levers, and the churning of her thirteen-bladed twenty-five-foot-wide wheel, all occasionally were drowned by the verte-brae-rattling blast of her steam-bellowing whistle. And her noise stifled even that of the *Queen*.

But the *Queen* was having none of it, and her pilot, Big Henry Slocumb, boldly swung her bow and closed with the larger craft as it neared the narrow channel entrance. Clint hooked a leg over the pommel of his saddle and watched the developing confrontation of steamboat wills and pilot hardheadedness with interest. Both boats roiled white water behind, seemingly mindless of the narrow seventy-foot opening to Som'bitch Slough ahead, but the crowd on the bow of the smaller *Queen* began to give way in fearful anticipation as the gap between the boats narrowed.

On each trip upriver the boats hosted a throng of argonauts, men in heavy boots laced to above their calves, wearing shirts of every color and hats of every description—some, such as the tassels dangling from the brims of the Peruvians', or the upside-down pot appearance of the Chileans', identifying the nationality of the owner.

Australians, Sandwich Island Kanakas, Filipinos, Chinese, Frenchmen, Mexicans, Italians, Brits, Americans—from every nook and cranny of the States—clung to the rails and balustrades or bellied up to the bars and gaming tables with packs and shovels and picks slung over their backs; shotguns and rifles in hand; belt hatchets, pistols, machetes, bowies, and Arkansas toothpicks sheathed or shoved through their belts. Men who had paid three dollars or more apiece for the salon deck or far more for a private stateroom, crowded the rails of each boat.

Clint had passed more than two hundred men on the trail—a few mounted on donkeys, mules, or horses, but most afoot—who had refused or could not afford three days wages. They preferred shank's mare and a hard two-and-a-half-day hike to the ten-hour, three-dollar steamship ride.

On each return trip downriver, the boats' decks echoed vacantly, but a six-hundred-pound safe in each purser's cabin was always several hundred pounds heavier than during the trip up—gold, in dust and nuggets.

The final approach to Som'bitch Slough lay wide enough for only one of the pair of boats that vied for the business between San Francisco and Sacramento City and the goldfields beyond, yet more than once the pilots of competing boats had aimed their bows for the same narrow space, and the devil take the hindmost. The derelict ribs of a hundred-footer, the *King of Persia,* still rested on the sand spit of Grand Island, where the slough rejoined the river, having been shoved aside by the *Ruler* six months before in the dead of fogbound winter. Twenty-six men had drowned in that catastrophe, even though she had grounded very near the southmost tip of Grand Island, formed between Steamboat Slough and the main river. But the water boiled around the island's point, and the upcurrent fifty feet from the bow of the *King of Persia* to solid land might as well have been a mile to all but the strongest swimmers.

With his attention welded to the impending fight for the narrows, Clint, normally wary, did not hear the man behind until a deep resonant voice began to berate him.

"This here is my part of the river, sinner. Unless you're here to be saved from your heathen ways, you whip up that ugly yellow crowbait and get back on the trail."

Clint rested his hand on the butt of his Colt's and shifted in the saddle to eye the speaker, but let it drop away when he noted the tall scarecrow of a man was unarmed.

He was dressed in patched black trousers

with river mud weighing down the cuffs, his sockless ankles showing between cuff and hightop shoes—their soles so thin he could have stood on a dollar and told if it was heads or tails—and a misshapen and disheveled swallowtail coat over a sweat-stained once-white shirt. He looked more the down-and-out hotel clerk than a threat, but still he continued his tirade while he slapped at his own clan of mosquitoes.

"Don't ya know, I said lay the whip on that knot-headed yellow horse, and move away!"

More irritated that the man had insulted Diablo than that he was chiding him, Clint ignored him. He was far more interested in the developing confrontation between the boats and was in little mood to flatten or even parlay with the man at the moment. But the gaunt-faced speaker did radiate a certain wildness from his eyes that caused Clint to give him more notice than he might have otherwise.

"I'll be moving on downriver in a moment. Soon as I watch these two boats pass."

"You'll move now!"

Clint glanced back at the approaching boats, now no more than two hundred yards from Som'bitch Slough's entrance. With the continued badgering, irritation began to harden to anger, and he eyed the man up and down once more. He appeared to be as tall as Clint, maybe taller, but thin and storklike, with a prominent Adam's apple vibrating in his loose-skinned turkey neck, a feature only overshadowed by black serpent's eyes and brooding salt-and-pepper brows. His hands were thin, too, but red and rawboned, and clenched at his sides where they protruded too far out of frayed sleeves.

"You're on the land of Rancho del Rio Ancho, friend," Clint said with a firm but friendly voice. "This is hardly 'your part of the shore,' so why don't you wander away and let me watch these boats in peace?" He noticed a small cotton twill tent in the background, as patched and ragged as the man's suit.

The man's eyes flared widely as he shook his fist up at the mounted rider. "By the Good Book, you'll ride away or I'll smite you down like Jehovah smote the Philistines."

Clint sighed deeply. It was too damned hot for this foolishness. "Every ass has a right to bray, friend," he said, his tone hardening. "But don't talk of smitin' unless you've got more sand than this river."

The man's eyes narrowed and he charged forward. Clint spun Diablo to face him, knocking the man aside when he did so. The scarecrow stumbled back and fell over his own feet, his long arms windmilling, then he plopped on his butt in the slimy mud among the tules. Both hands sunk up to bony wrists.

He screamed at Clint as if he had been dropped in hot oil. "You heathen! You've caused me to soil my suit. I'll have your—"

Before he could finish, the wrenching crash of timber caused both men to whip their attention to the river. The *Queen* had not given way and had crashed into the bigger boat. With her bow splintered, she lurched from the charging *Ruler.* Clint stared in horror. The *Queen* heeled over like a small sailing sloop under full canvas, and careened aside, her bow taking water, her sidewheel smashed but still churning and throwing splintered paddle arms like kindling. Through momentum alone, she bore down on the point of Grand Island where her former competitor, the *King of Persia,* lay, now only a haunting derelict skeleton, devoid of skin or innards.

The men on the *Queen*'s deck had been thrown together in piles; cursing, thrashing legs, kicking and struggling, they fought to regain their dignity and their feet. A few unfortunates were flung into the water. A dozen mules, whose small on-deck corral had been shattered by their weight on impact, slid into and smashed through, or jumped over, the rail.

The *Ruler* charged on into the slough, unmindful of the drama unfolding in her wake, her stout bulwark only slightly marked. The California Steam Navigation Company and their mighty *River Ruler* had prevailed again.

Just when the *Queen* began to right herself and the men on board regained their feet, she furrowed onto the hidden sand spit off the point of Grand Island, plowing until she smashed into the skeleton of the *King of Persia*. She did a slow roll, dumping more men and cargo overboard while her stern swung out into the powerful main course of the river. Just when she seemed about to stabilize, the current caught her stern and drove it back. She righted, only to heel over to the other rail. Men and cargo that had not tumbled over her starboard rails now crashed over, or through, her port side.

Clint loosed his rawhide reata from its ties on the forks of the saddle, shook out a loop, and gave his heels to the big horse. Diablo plunged forward, guided by knees alone, following the riverbank downstream. More than a half-hundred men fought and flailed to reach the shore, some clinging to crates and barrels, some to mule's tails or manes, and many of them beginning to fail in the effort. A hundred feet downstream, Clint's reata flashed sixty feet out into the stream and dropped over a man whose mouth was opened wide enough in screaming terror to see his backbone. He grasped the line just as another swimmer reached him and held on. Clint spun the stallion up away from the river, dallied quickly, and the horse dragged the men out of the water.

Clint yelled at the men to shed the loop, then repeated the process, managing to snag two more swimmers. Again he recoiled quickly, and glanced back upriver. The *Queen* lay over at a thirty-degree angle, which would not have been so bad had it not been for the fact that her boilers roared on, still billowing black smoke out of her stack. Clint had been aboard many a steamship and, being an ex-sailor, had been interested in their operation. He knew her askew boilers would only hold for a short time with the flues inside not covered with water. They would quickly become red-hot, and boiler pressure would rise almost instantaneously.

Almost as soon as he had the thought, she exploded, blowing splintered timber and cargo and men in great arcs, pursued by clouds of scalding steam, then by a billowing storm of fire. Self-preservation an instinct, Clint spun Diablo, drove his spurs in the horse's sides, and hunkered low in the saddle. Diablo's powerful hindquarters kicked mud behind and carried them up the riverbank. Something struck Clint in the back, but did not dislodge him from the saddle. Smoking debris dropped around them for the first fifty yards of the wild ride, then stopped. Clint reined up and turned back to the scene below.

The *Queen* was afire. Flotsam, including bodies and body parts, floated away with the current. Clint took a deep steadying breath, then gigged the stallion back down the slope.

To his surprise, he noted that the black-suited scarecrow had boarded a small catboat, one he must have had hidden in the tules, and was busily rowing about shouting incantations of biblical reference, but all the while gathering up survivors.

Again at the shore, Clint tossed his loop and snagged another man, who floated facedown in the river. He spun Diablo and dragged the load out of the water only to realize he had rescued only half a man. He spurred back and leaped out of the saddle to free the loop from its grizzly load, trying not to look at the raw carnage of what remained of the argonaut. Refusing to acknowledge his own churning stomach, Clint remounted and tossed the loop at a man who fought the current, and hauled three more ashore while others clung to him. Clint recognized the man he had snagged. Big Henry Slocumb; the *Queen*'s pilot and a man who regularly made the newspapers for his antics. Slocumb's flowing red beard frizzed black, half burned away, but he seemed undaunted. As he shed the loop he cursed the *Ruler* rather than his own ineptitude, and made no offer of thanks to the man who had pulled him from the brown swirls of the Sacramento.

"By the saints, I'll skewer Ezekiel Hammond on his own boom and display him the length of the channel." he raved. The brawny pilot continued to shout and wave his arms, assuring the scorched and bruised men gathering on shore of how wronged, not wrong, he had been.

Clint shook his head with disgust and went back to his task. He knew that Big Henry Slocumb and Ezekiel Hammond were the most highly paid pilots on the river—probably the highest-paid workers in California—rumored to be making the astronomical sum of two thousand dollars a month, and wondered how men making that much money and having that much responsibility could be so intemperate and reckless with their trusts.

Clint, the scarecrow preacher, and many of the men who had made shore—some of them badly scalded—continued to work well into the night, their efforts lighted by the fire aboard the *Queen* while what was left of her burned down to the waterline. Clint noticed that Big Henry Slocumb slipped quietly away into the darkness when the men on shore began to grumble and place the blame where it belonged.

At dawn bodies lined the banks, debris cluttered the tules and river willows and hung from the branches of a few cottonwoods that rose from the shores. Wisps of smoke rose in the still morning air from what had been a grand boat and was now little more than a memory.

The quiet was broken only by the moans of scalded, scorched, water-laden men. A squadron of small boats finally arrived from Sacramento City, bearing crews of rescuers, who pitched in, loading the injured, collecting the dead, and trying to salvage what freight they could. Clint dropped to a log, exhausted both mentally and physically. The man whom he had had the confrontation with had been working equally hard through the night, and walked over and sat beside him.

"Looks like 'your part of the shore' got a little crowded," Clint managed.

"'Tis the Lord's work we've done this night, and you're welcome to stay here for a while and bask in His glory."

"I'd just as soon not bask in this particular glory, pilgrim." Clint shook his head in wonderment at the man for a moment. Finally he stood and walked over to recover Diablo from where he had tied him to a willow. Without comment, he brushed the big horse's back down then swung the blanket and saddle into place and cinched it up. He bridled, untied and coiled the lead rope and tied it to the pommel, then mounted. Looking out over the scene, he noted with satisfaction some boats loaded with salvaged cargo and injured men moving out upstream.

There was nothing more he could do here, and he was already a day late for his appointment at the hacienda of Don Carlos Vega—and Don Carlos would not have called him from so far if he did not have a serious problem.

Clint tipped his wide-brimmed palo alto hat at the scarecrow. "You can have it, pilgrim. Bask away." He swung the big stallion away and did not bother to turn back when he heard the man call after him.

"You come back anytime, stranger."

But Clint decided he had seen enough of riverboat races to last him a good long time, and basking with the scarecrow was not his idea of a good way to wile away an afternoon. He urged Diablo into a lope.

"There's a little grain and rest ahead," he assured the big horse.

Already the morning heat was beginning to work at them, and the mosquitoes were back in clan-force clouds.

2

Rachel DuBois reclined on Garth Hutchinson's daybed—kept in his office because many nights he only paused for a few hours' sleep. Purposely exposing just a little more stockinged ankle than at all proper, she glanced up over the *San Francisco Call* as he moved from his desk to the shuttered window and leaned out to view Long Wharf. San Francisco's most impressive boat landing stretched out from Garth's land's-end office for almost six hundred feet into the bay.

Garth had leased the primely located office on the same day he had passed through the Golden Gate, so christened by the explorer John Frémont only three years before while the bay was still a Mexican possession and while San Francisco was still known as Yerba Buena. The tall Hutchinson was able to lean far out, as he had not bothered to have the shuttered window glazed. Instead, all of his money was going into refurbishing the *Benicia Belle*, tied up at the wharf below. Rachel smiled, noting that Garth's thick shoulders filled the window. He turned back and winked at her as he silently crossed the Chinese-silk carpet to his massive cypress desk.

"She's coming along fine. They're hauling the tables and chairs into the main salon now. We're ahead of schedule."

Rachel returned the wink and brushed her long black tresses back out of her eyes while holding his admiring gaze. When he went back to his paperwork, she returned to the newspaper.

The handsome Easterner had lured her away from a very profitable job as a singer at the Eldorado, San Francisco most successful drinking-and-gambling establishment, with the promise of an even more profitable job on board the *Belle* and with a suite at the Palace. And she had been ready, far more so than she had let him believe. She had worked long and hard and needed a few days' respite. The *Belle* was not due to be rechristened for another week, and all Rachel had to do in the meantime was visit the ladies who would sew

19

her costumes and clothes or fashion her hats.

He had also lured her with the hint of a relationship that might go far beyond that of employer and employee, and had, in fact, attempted to demonstrate that intent with a heated advance during her first night in the suite. But she had repelled his assault as surely as Travis had repelled the first attacks on the Alamo, and that battle was a good comparison, for she knew she would succumb as surely as the Alamo had, a victim of superior force—or so she would let him believe. Then she would receive her reparations. But in good time, in good time.

Her mother had raised no fool.

Rachel admired Garth Hutchinson and was sure she could come to love him, but that was less important. He had brought the *Belle*, then christened the *Algonquin*, and sailed her all the way round Terra del Fuego to California from the Hudson River, stopping in Charleston, where he had her fitted out with the best of fine-grained cypress bars and back bars, tables and chairs, full-length mirrors and crystal chandeliers—fitted, then packed away again. The fine furniture and fixtures had remained deep in her holds, stored in crates, while the proud boat had been almost crated up herself. Every window and hold had been battened down, and even her lathe-turned rails and balustrades had been planked over, preparing for the often fatal passage around the cape.

As it turned out, the trip around Tierra del Fuego was almost that, but the *Belle,* beaten, battered, and waterlogged, survived.

Reaching Valparaiso, Chile, Garth had opened her two hundred ten feet of deck space to receive passengers, and from there to Callao, Peru; Guayaquil, Ecuador; Panama City, Panama; San Juan del Sur, Nicaragua; San José, Guatemala; and Acapulco de Juarez, Mexico, he had gathered paying fares. Anyone who had the money could ride in Spartan accommodations on the decks—for all available hold and cabin space had been packed with goods to be sold in supply- hungry California.

By the time he left Panama City he had already regained his investment in the boat and her refitting; by the time he arrived in San Francisco and sold the goods to a variety of stores, he was a hundred thousand dollars in the black from passage money and profit on freight. And it was a good thing he was, for he had a spare engine stowed in her holds and two new and very unique boilers. They had to be in place and the boat rigged before her first run up the river, and that would take big money. He made the passage on her one reliable old engine and boiler and would wait for the quiet of San Francisco's protected harbor before he tried his experiment—twin engines and a complicated system of gears.

Now even that refitting had been accomplished, and soon they would give her a trial run.

Rachel stretched and yawned, but got no notice from Garth. It would not do to spend so much time near him that he tired of her, and she had been in his office for almost an hour. She folded the paper and rose.

"I'm off to the milliner's," she said, smoothing her yellow silk faille dress.

"Hold on a minute," he said, not lifting his eyes from the paperwork.

"I need to get some new bonnets fitted and trimmed—"

"There, I'm finished." He laid the quill aside, looked up, focused deep blue eyes, and flashed one of those devastating smiles that had gained him so much. And what they had not gained from others, his powerful shoulders and thick arms had accomplished. "I want you to take a walk through the *Belle* with me. The hatter can wait."

"But Garth, there's only one milliner in San Fran—"

"I'll brook no argument, even from the most beautiful woman on the continent. You need to see in what fine style you'll be traveling and where you'll be singing. Besides, who wouldn't wait on you?"

He rose and moved around the desk. It always amazed her how a man so large and powerful could move so lightly. His carriage was as smooth as his tongue. He offered her his arm, and in feigned irritation she accepted, but she felt the same warm twinge when she rested her head on his rock-hard forearm that she had when she had first looked into those blue eyes a week before in the Eldorado.

A large black man waited on the landing outside and, as they passed, fell in a few steps behind. The man was thick of chest and an ax handle wide, with wide features that displayed no emotion.

They moved down the narrow stairway to the heavy planks of the wharf. Men happily singing a sea chantey as they labored glanced up and saw them coming. The singing faded.

As always when she moved about the streets of San Francisco, the workingmen stopped and stared. Women of any ilk were a scarcity in San Francisco, and a woman of Rachel's incredible beauty was virtually nonexistent. And she was fully aware of it. For a fleeting moment she thought the men had stopped their enthusiastic song because Garth Hutchinson was on the dock, but that was silly. Everyone knew that men who sang while they worked got more done. Garth would have approved. No, it was because she had appeared that they stopped, she decided.

Even Garth, who normally would have barked an order to return to work, did not seem to mind when the men hesitated and looked up, none daring to stare while she was on his arm, but all casting furtive admiring glances. The couple mounted the gangplank and moved to the main deck of the *Belle*, then up another level to the Texas deck, where the main salon was being finished. With a gallant bow, Garth swung aside the batwing doors and bade her enter.

Rachel gasped. When she had first seen

24

the boat two weeks before, its salon was barren as her own purse had been when she had first arrived in the city. Now prism-covered chandeliers hung from copper-molded ceilings, green-and-purple velvet-covered chairs and settees lined the walls, and gambling tables for fan-tan, poker, roulette, faro, and other games stood in green felt splendor around the main room. At the far end, a fine polished cypress bar and back bar stood regally in place, and men labored stocking it. Mirrors, some as tall as seven feet, which cost a phenomenal sum, bracketed the bar and lined the walls nearby. The balance of the walls stood bedecked with thick drapes or windowed with four-by-six-foot openings, each with a dozen small but precious one-by-two-foot glass panes. Chinese carpets of silk and Persian carpets of fine wool covered the polished mahogany decks.

"I can't believe what you've accomplished, Garth." Rachel gave him a smile to match his best. Her emerald eyes widened in appreciation of the room, and of the handsome man who beamed back at her.

"Where there's a will . . ." He let the sentence fade as he saw something displeasing. "By the saints!" he snapped, then yelled at a man across the wide room: "O'Flarraty, get over here!"

A squat man hurried across the room, snatched his floppy- brimmed hat off his head, exposing its gleaming baldness, and stopped in front of his boss.

"I told you I wanted the Kentucky whiskeys to line the back bar and the liqueurs and other whiskeys on the second shelf and above."

"I'm no bartender," the little man groused, then immediately regretted doing so. His already blotched face flushed a solid red and he mopped at the sweat on his pate and dropped his eyes.

Garth Hutchinson's lips thinned, his jaw knotted, and his shoulders seemed to hunker forward as if he were ready to pounce on the little man. Then he glanced at Rachel and collected himself. When he returned his attention to the man, he said in a steady voice, "Unless you're ready to collect your miserable pay, Stubby, you'll be whatever I *say* you'll be."

"Yes, sir. I'm sorry, Mr. Hutchinson, it's just that we're working damn—" The man cut his eyes to Rachel, then he reddened a deeper shade, almost as purple as the chair upholstery. "I'm . . . sorry . . . ma'am. We're not . . . not used to having—"

"Get back to work. you miserable mick. The next time you'll be down the plank."

The little Irishman's face hardened, but his words belied his expression. "There'll be no next time, Mr. Hutchinson. I'm sorry, ma'am." He could hardly hurry away fast enough.

Garth's smile returned as he moved back to Rachel's side. "The damned Irish are the worst of the lot. If I had my way . . ."

Rachel gave him a bit of a disappointed glance at the way he had treated the man, but then realized that Garth had gotten an incredible amount done and she could hardly fault his methods. He had given her a long lecture at dinner one night shortly after she had moved into the suite, informing her that his employees admired and respected him, and would do anything for him. She had believed him, but now offered, "You've been working these men night and day."

"Yes, I have, and will until she's right, then the California Steam Navigation Company and their so-called *River Ruler* will learn what competition, the *Benicia*

27

Belle, and Garth Hutchinson are all about. The *Belle* will be the real queen of the river and the *Ruler* only a prince . . . if that."

Rachel smiled, knowing that he too had been working day and night. "You'll do it, I've no doubt," she said, taking his arm as he led her back out on the deck. She once more extolled the virtues of the main salon on their way down to the main deck. Wherever they went, the big hulking black followed a few steps behind.

"Now you'll see the thing I'm most proud of." He beamed and opened a door carrying a brass sign embossed ENGINE ROOM.

Stretching before her lay a space twenty paces long and half as many wide, jammed full of machinery and pipes—and stiflingly hot. Rachel had no idea, and less interest, in what she was seeing, but Garth grinned like a little boy with his first pocketknife.

"Two, Rachel! Not one, but two steam engines. New boilers of my own design, thirty feet long and only three feet wide. More surface area to create steam," he exclaimed, and she shook her head as if it all made sense. "And most importantly, each side wheel is independent of the other."

She smiled and nodded her head, but it was clear to him that she did not understand the value of this innovative approach.

"So she can turn not only with her rudder, but with the aid of her paddle wheels . . . turn in her own length!" He carefully explained, and waited for her look of astonishment. She tried to keep the perplexed look off her face, but was obviously unsuccessful, then became far more concerned with the heat in the confined space.

"You're melting my makeup, Garth."

He continued as he showed her back out to the main deck. "One wheel can actually be reversed, and this boat, like no other," he repeated, "should be able to turn in her own length. A fantastic accomplishment. And we can run on only one engine! Should one fail, the survivor can be geared to drive both wheels."

She forced another smile, beginning to become bored and worrying about her milliner's appointment, which now really was growing near. "It's wonderful, Garth, but I really must get on. . . . I hope you've paid half so much attention to my dressing room and quarters."

"Those I'll show you only when I've finished," he said, his look fading from disappointment to mischievousness. He turned his attention away and waved across the deck. The man he had assigned to watch over her, the black who towered even above the tall Garth Hutchinson, waited a respectful distance away.

"Joshua!" Garth snapped, and his slave quickstepped over and snatched his hat off his gallon-keg head.

"Yes'er."

"Miss DuBois has an appointment. Take the carriage and drive her. And be damned careful or I'll stripe your hide."

"Yes'er."

Rachel smiled at Garth, waved condescendingly to him, then impatiently to Joshua, and led the hulking man away.

Garth fished a long nine out of his waistcoat pocket, drew a sulfur head across the strike patch on the box, lit up, and watched her walk away. She was a fine-looking woman—as fine as they came—and even though she did not have the voice of a nightingale, she had a hundred times the beauty of the most regal bird and would be just one more of the many attractions that would pry the river business away from the California Steam Navigation Company. And his hundred thousand dollars, rapidly being diminished by the expense of finishing out the *Belle* and setting up the office and dock space in both Sacramento and San Francisco, and the wood stop along the route, would become a million in no time.

God willing, he and the *Belle* would rule the river soon.

Clint could have cut across country and reached the hacienda a little sooner, but he liked the river and wanted to follow it as long as he could. It meant he had to fight the occasional marsh, cross a few sloughs, and battle a constant barrage of mosquitoes, but he also enjoyed the geese, ducks, herons, stilts, egrets, and hundreds of other water birds that roamed or soared over the tules.

The old *carreta* trail to Don Carlos Vega's compound left the river from a landing at Honker Bay. At Honker and Suisun and Grizzly bays, the waterway widened to what was really a series of shallow but expansive lakes, then narrowed again at Carquinez Straights before dumping into San Pablo Bay. San Pablo, as brackish as its continuation, San Francisco Bay, was where the ocean truly began.

Clint loved the sea, loved the smell of it, the beauty and the fury. He had spent twelve years on the world's great oceans before being shipwrecked north of Santa Barbara. A wreck that had brought him to California—and one he now, in a strange way, considered propitious, for he loved California as much as he had the sea.

He was learning to care particularly for the great delta area where the Sacramento worked its way through California's central valley and merged with the smaller San Joaquin, Calaveras, and Mokelumne rivers and the confluence of valley-bottom sloughs formed from many rivers originating farther south in the Sierras—all of which dumped into the great and nearly impassable wetlands that filled the wide fertile rift between the Sierras and the coast range. At Carquinez Straights, the river broached the coast range of mountains and fresh water met salt. The great push of water, still carrying the cold of snow from fourteen-thousand-foot-high mountains, clashed with the equally unrelenting tidal force of the world's largest ocean, the Pacific. The Pacific entered the central valley with its brackish salt water via an eight-knot tidal rush, through the narrow Golden Gate into wide San Francisco Bay, then north into San Pablo Bay before clashing with the snow-cold fresh at the straights.

As if that confluence of ocean and great river at Carquinez wasn't wild and roiling enough, the Napa River came in from the north at almost the same spot to add to the confusing tempest of fresh and salt.

The area inland, above the Carquinez and on the edge of the river bays, was a maze of sloughs and smaller creeks, mud flats and channels. Tules and occasional stretches of willows and cottonwoods rose in the few spots where solid ground offered root hold.

Salmon ran all the rivers and sturgeon cruised their depths, nourishing Miwok, Maidu, Wintun, Yocuts, Pomo, and Costanoan Indian tribes who had claimed the shores for many thousands of years and who now tenuously shared the waterways —bays, sloughs, rivers, and creeks, which were the essence of their way of life—with thousands of argonauts moving across into the goldfields of the Sierra. Argonauts who used the waterways and shores only for transportation and cared little whose land they crossed or who claimed its bounty.

Cattle, too, roamed among the tules, cattle that belonged to the Mexican dons who had claimed the land for the last two hundred years.

And all was observed by deer and tule elk and black bear and otters and muskrats and millions of waterfowl—and the king of it all, the mighty grizzly.

Nature's forces and man's cultures clashed in the delta. Water against water, mountain tempest against ocean squall as winds met and mixed. Mexican against Anglo, Mexican against Mexican, Anglo against Anglo—and all men of all colors against the red man, the only one of the cornucopia of mankind living in harmony with nature's force.

If that were not enough, there were also men from a hundred nations of the world, with only one goal in mind—gold. And the devil take the hindmost and whoever dared stand in their way.

Clint had been ashore for the last five years and had witnessed great changes in the state—a Mexican territory when he first wandered into Pueblo Santa Barbara after a stay with the Chumash Indians, who found him nearly dead, washed ashore on a long stretch of beach. And he helped in the revolution, when the United States beat the Mexicans, though he smiled when he thought of it and heard pompous tales of glory extolled by the few Anglos who had participated. The Mexicans won every major battle in the revolution, and only their own internal strife and lack of organization beat them—at least in California. He had seen her seventh flag, the Bear Flag, rise over a declared republic, replaced only nineteen days later by the Stars and Stripes. All of California—the Mexicans and the Americans—had been against the seventh flag, with the exception of the few men who declared their independence and raised the banner over Sonoma. But it had lived on as the guidon of John Frémont and his regiment, the Bears, or *Los Osos,* as the Mexicans knew them, and now flew as the new state's flag.

Clint had not come through it all unscathed. He had learned well, and still wore the *calzonevas,* narrow-legged chaps buttoned with silver conchos down their split sides. They doubled as pants in the summer and covered wool pants in winter. He wore the flat-brimmed hat of the Mexican don. A short jacket, *charro,* lay tied in his bedroll, a reata was tied to his saddle. Clint carried the scars of more than one wound and still worried about an American warrant for his arrest that had been issued by Counsel Thomas Larkin while California was still Mexican territory. The warrant was requested by the captain of the wrecked brig *Savannah,* accusing Clint of malfeasance and dereliction of duty, but was actually a smoke screen covering the captain's own ineptitude. As far as Clint knew, that warrant remained active, though he had helped Commodore Stockton during the revolution with the promise that the officer would help get the document recalled. Stockton had been a busy man the last time Clint had seen him, with Clint's problem the last thing on his mind. Clint hoped the warrant was long forgotten. Still, it was a problem that gnawed at him like a dog at a day-old bone, particularly now that he wanted to become a landowner.

But now all of California was in turmoil, mayhem brought on by gold and its inevitable consequence—greed.

Clint drew rein as he topped a little rise and looked down on the widening river and Honker Bay. The last time he had been here Don Carlos Vega's landing had been only a sand spit. Now four dozen men worked extending a pier out into the bay near the main current of the Sacramento and a half-dozen oxen-pulled *carretas* were being un-loaded near huge stacks of firewood. The stacks grew where tules had once been. A flat scow workboat with a derrick on its prow and a donkey steam engine on its stern raised a heavy timber battering ram that hung ten feet through its derrick guides, falling to drive a pier post into the mud below. Its fifteen-second- interval dull thuds reminded Clint that he was witness-ing progress. Clint gigged the stallion down the slope, reined up, and dismounted.

Men moved about busily, ignoring him, as Clint tied the palomino to a river wil-low then studied the crew—Californians, Chinese, and a few Miwok Indians—to see if he recognized any of Don Carlos's old vaqueros. Finally, he spotted Sancho Gui-terrez, Rancho del Rio Ancho's head va-quero and the don's *segundo*, second in command and foreman, who stood, arms folded in obvious disgust, directing the un-loading and stacking of firewood.

Clint walked over, folded his arms, and waited until Sancho was finished berating a crew for the way the wood stack was pro-gressing.

He finally glanced over. His face breaking into a wide grin, Sancho shoved the som-

37

brero back off his head to rest on his back, strode over, and extended a gnarled hand. "El Lazo, I thought you would come."

Sancho called him by his vaquero nickname, El Lazo, the lasso—a name gained only after Clint had worked long and hard to learn the skills of the vaquero, and had proved his proficiency.

"Don Carlos sets a fine table, amigo. Nothing could have kept me away." They shared a laugh before Clint continued. "Gideon is watching over the *caballos* down on the Kaweah, horses I would not have were it not for the don. How could I not come?"

"You earned those horses, amigo," the vaquero said with a smile, then his face hardened. "Don Carlos does need your help, but Apolonia and I had to convince him to call on you. He is still hardheaded and, if he had his way, would ask no man for aid."

"The message asked only that I come. What's the problem?"

"That is for him to say, but I will ride back with you. Now, if you are ready." There was no humor in Sancho's tone or expression, and Clint knew that whatever troubled the old don must be serious.

He walked back to Diablo, mounted, and

38

wheeled the horse around to join Sancho just as five scrubby-looking men, their skimpy belongings on their backs, moved afoot down the low hill and stopped in front of the vaquero. Clint urged Diablo over next to the Rancho del Rio Ancho *segundo,* who listened intently and politely while the largest of the group spoke—*large,* with shoulders door-filling big and a girth as thick as deep, was an understatement.

"We need us some work to tide us over on our way to the diggin's," he said, his voice booming and confident. "We'll just set to helping those fellas on the derrick boat and get to planking this quay. God knows they need help by the looks of the miserable lot. An' two dollars a day for the boys here and three for me will suit us fine. When's payday?"

Clint could not help but admire the man's forward manner—an assumptive job application if he ever saw one—but he knew Sancho Guiterrez well and knew how poorly the gringo's approach would be received even before the *segundo* opened his mouth. Hat in hand might have gotten the men a job.

"We have all the help we need," Sancho snapped. "Stay on the river trail as you move through Rancho del Rio Ancho and you are welcome to pass. The cattle belong to Don Carlos Vega and he would take great offense at their harm." Sancho reined his horse away.

"Hold up there, greaser, are you claimin' we be cow thieves?" their leader snarled, and spat a great gob of tobacco spittle onto the sand.

Clint could see Sancho's expression harden. The vaquero spun the horse back and slipped from the saddle in an easy motion. He looked like a banty rooster facing a badger. Clint urged Diablo between the two men almost as soon as Sancho hit the ground. The *segundo* was better than fifty years old, and would give away a hundred pounds and twenty years to the bigger man—not to speak of the fact that Sancho was unarmed and his opponent carried an eighteen-inch Arkansas toothpick and a smaller camp knife stuffed in his belt.

Clint noticed the wide-faced man's eyebrows had been split and healed in twenty places, his nose angled in three directions, and his cheekbones were a spiderweb of scars on scars. This was a man who had bumped heads in many a back alley.

"And who might you be, friend?" Clint

asked quietly, leaning forward in the saddle.

"Who might I be!" His voice boomed. He threw back his head and roared in laughter, then rested his hamlike fists on his ample waist. Clint, long a judge of men, knew it was muscle not fat that thickened it.

The man's four friends, equally rough looking if not so oversized, smiled, dropped back out of the way, shed their packs, and folded their arms in relaxed interest, as if they knew what was coming from long experience.

"Who might I be," he repeated. "Why, man, you must be daft not to know Bob 'Boulders' Blanchard, the toughest keelboat hand ever to pollywog all the way up the Nile and down the Amazon. Alone, I could cordelle that work scow up the Niagara Falls, then stand on the top and outpiss 'er. I've whipped every cock o' the walk and root hog from Cairo—Illinois, that is—to the Golden Gate, right afore I swilled they whiskey, et they grub, and stood stud to they women, and I'm a-workin' my way up to Sacramento City at the moment, where, I might add"—and his gaze drilled into Sancho—"I intend to service me a bevy of them greaser girlies and add a little sinew to a sorry strain."

He threw off his hat, exposing shoulder-length mouse-brown hair surrounding a bald pate, and began unbuttoning his linsey-woolsey shirt, beneath which lay a thatch of hair to match that on his head. The hat had had a fine place to sit—both of the tops of the man's ears were bitten off in a jagged tooth-marked line. His tangle of brown hair flared askew like a bison's, and he reminded Clint of a drawing a Greek sailor had made of a heavily muscled satyr—albeit one with hobnailed boots rather than cloven boots. Boulders paced while he roared on, addressing the few men who had stopped their work to stare.

"I'm hard as the hubs of hell and twice as hot! Mama was an alligator and daddy a swamp panther. I got balls like boulders, hence the name. I'll turn your toes up faster than a rattler can strike and surer than the cholera."

When Boulders cast his shirt aside, Clint noticed a dozen blades had carved marks on his chest, back, and knotted arms, which he folded as he took a wide stance and turned his attention back to Sancho.

"Now, I'll ask one more time afore I start

42

waltzin' my way through you poor excuses for the fruit of Adam's loins. I got men here who want to work and the best crew boss on God's green earth to push 'em! When the hell's payday?"

The men in Sancho's work crew and even the men on the pier had stopped working and had begun to gather around while Boulders Blanchard roared on. Clint studied the bellowing man. He knew riverboat men had the reputation of liking to fight more than to eat or drink, and no riverboat man was said to be worth a pound of salt unless he had at least one ear bitten off. Boulders seemed worth two pounds or more.

Sancho Guiterrez worked his way around Diablo and stood somewhat in amazement at the gringo who prattled away. Clint eyed the two men, now only six feet apart, and decided this was not going to come to an easy end.

"You gonna shuck those knives?" Clint asked evenly, resting his own hand on the Colt's at his hip.

Blanchard looked up and grinned widely. "I'll take you on two atta time with blades or bludgeons, or with the paltry fists an' them bony feet the Good Lord cursed you

43

with, friend!" His eyes narrowed. "But having my way, it'll be bungholes an' elbows, gouge, bite, kick, an' holler, an' we'll leave the blades to lesser men." He grinned again. "If they be any lesser'n you."

"Shuck the knives," Clint said simply, throwing a leg over the pommel and slipping from the saddle without turning his back on the man. He unbuckled his gunbelt and hung it on the horn, running his own ten-inch knife alongside the Colt's into its holster.

Blanchard guffawed at this turn of events. "Why, you skinny runt, I believe I knewed the sorry mama goat what gave you naught but the dry hind tit." Boulders ignored Sancho and squared away with Clint, his hands still at rest on his wide hips. "I hauled her and the rest of her flock from St. Joe to Natchez. I'll give you this, she was the prettiest of the lot, and she bleated a fine song. But she musta forgot to write . . . I didn't know we had us a young'n."

His friends roared in laughter, slapping their thighs. Clint felt the heat rush to his neck and shrugged off the arm Sancho laid on his shoulder.

"This is my problem, amigo," the vaquero said from behind him.

44

Clint's eyes never left the big riverman's. "It's mine now, Sancho. Mr. Blanchard here has chosen to personalize it. Just keep the others off us."

"Others!" Blanchard said, roaring in laughter and throwing his head back again —which proved a mistake as Clint stepped in quick and drove a hard right under his upraised chin. The blow cracked like sledge on rock, snapped his head back, and the man windmilled his arms in surprise and landed on his beefy rump in the sand.

To Clint's chagrin, as he'd hit him hard enough to rock Clint to his own boots, the man shook his head like a bull poleaxed with a timber, then gazed up and smiled. Clint glanced around. The man's friends did not seem concerned, and Clint suddenly got even more so. He sailed his flat-brimmed hat away, deciding he had his work cut out for him.

Blanchard shook his head and struggled to his feet. "Why, boy, you butt like your grandpa, and like I did his'n, I'll eat yer oysters if'n you got any, and you'll end up mutton an' tater stew." He roared in laughter again, and again threw his head back, but this time wisely well out of striking range.

Clint rubbed his bruised knuckles and circled the man. "You make plenty of chin music with that alligator mouth, but do damn little marchin'. Let's get you river-scum-suckin' goat lovers whipped. We have important things to do."

Blanchard's eyes narrowed, his jaw knotted, and his lips went white and thin. He heated and glowered as if he'd been honed on a whetstone and tempered in hot oil.

Butterflies ticked Clint's innards as he waited for the charge he knew was coming.

Boulders pawed like one of the rancho's herd bulls and charged with the same confidence, fully intending to run right over his sandy-haired opponent.

Clint feinted then dropped and rolled, entangling Blanchard's legs with his as he passed, a trick he had learned from his mates on shipboard. Blanchard went down hard and sprawled in a cloud of dust. Clint leaped to his feet at the same time the big man came up, and drove two quick punches to his face. Blood squirted from an eyebrow and Blanchard backhanded it while Clint gave a backstep and judged him.

Then Blanchard grinned. "Yer quick, but that won't work again, you nanny-born ninny." He charged with flailing arms.

Clint ducked and one powerful right glanced off. Then he drove a fist deep into the man's belly as he passed. But he left it an instant too long as Blanchard's ham-like hand closed over his wrist. Hanging on to Clint's right with his left, Blanchard landed a crashing blow to the side of Clint's head that snapped it back, rocking him and almost doubling his knees. Clint ducked the next one and dived in, driving his head into Blanchard's midsection and at the same time twisting against the man's thumb and freeing the wrist.

Clint shook his head murkily as he backed away—he'd never been hit so hard by man or mule.

Again the two men squared off. Clint knew he was in for trouble if he allowed the larger man to get hold of him again with that viselike grip. Clint shook off the remnants of the blow to his head and gauged Blanchard's next charge. Sidestepping, he marked the man's spiderweb cheek with a straight left and clubbed him with a round-house right as he passed, splitting what was left of Blanchard's left ear.

The man faced him again, bleeding from eye, cheek, and ear. Clint gained confidence until he heard one of Blanchard's men offer two-to-one odds on a five-dollar gold piece, then another offer of three to one in favor of his trailmate.

Again Blanchard charged. Clint tried to drop and tangle his legs again, but Blanchard, true to his word, was not fooled and dived sideways, trapping Clint under his bulk. Both men rolled, punched, kneed, and elbowed, trying to gain the advantage. Blanchard angled to drive a thick thumb into Clint's eye. Clint dived away, but Blanchard was on him, cat quick and bull strong, grabbing Clint from behind in a bear hug, coiled steel arms locked around his chest, dragging him to his feet.

"That's all!" Clint overheard Blanchard's men again. "Four to one, boys!" one of them shouted.

The powerful man lifted Clint off his feet, beginning to squeeze the breath out of him, then racked him up and down. He tried to gnaw Clint's ear—the mark of the riverman—but Clint slammed his head back, smashing the man's nose.

Clint brought a booted heel down on Blanchard's instep and the riverman's grip weakened, then Clint kicked back and scraped his heel down the man's shin as he slammed him down again.

Blanchard tried to adjust his grip from around the chest to a killing grip around Clint's throat, but Clint managed to turn to face Blanchard—who still had a death grip around his chest that trapped one arm. Still smiling, Blanchard grunted and reddened in the face as he squeezed—and Clint head-butted him, smacking forehead to nose again and again until Blanchard's grip loosened and Clint was able to free his trapped arm.

Now Clint was able to flail him with blows to both sides of the head, and he pounded as quick and hard as he could, knocking Blanchard's massive head back and forth. But Blanchard just continued to squeeze and absorb the punishment, knowing Clint's breath would soon go. Even though he was taking a beating and bleeding from both eyes, ears, and cheekbones, he knew his opponent would soon pass out.

Clint knew it, too, when his vision fogged and began to fade. With a burst of fear-driven strength, he brought both hands wide and slammed the flat of callused palms against Blanchard's chowdered ears. The big man's eyes flared and he grimaced in pain, and Clint pounded again and again, great coordinated slapping blows that echoed over the sand spit, bringing his palms against the man's ear holes until Blanchard flung him away and grasped in

50

pain at his howling, and possibly broken, eardrums with both hands.

Clint sucked for wind, but didn't wait and stepped in, knocking Blanchard back with a powerful right to the man's crooked nose, which sprayed blood like a faucet. But Blanchard hooked a right that staggered Clint, then a left, then another right—all hammering sledge blows as telling as the first one had been.

Clint's head swam and he stumbled away, trying to avoid the man's onrush, ducking under him, but Blanchard brought an uppercut into his midsection, then jerked Clint's linsey-woolsey shirt over his head and hammered again and again at Clint's solar plexus. Clint saw red, then realized he was on the ground, doubled up, covering his vitals, expecting the hammer of booted feet—but none came.

Clint fought for consciousness. He shook off the clouds and peered around for his adversary. Then he realized that Sancho had stepped into the fray and was trading blows with the big riverman—and getting by far the worst of it.

With fear for his old friend and a surge of strength, Clint gathered his legs under him and drove forward, catching Blanchard behind the knees and doubling him over.

Blanchard went down and Clint rolled away and managed to drag himself to his feet.

Sancho kicked the rising riverman square in the face with a booted foot, snapping his head, knocking him to his back. But the man rolled and regained his feet, back-handing the blood away and grinning.

"Now the odds is about right," he said, eyeing both Clint and Sancho. None of his men made a move to help him, and Clint was convinced Blanchard was not just bragging.

Clint managed to get his breath, but he realized Sancho was hurt, bleeding from a split eye and ear and favoring a leg.

"Hold . . . up," Clint said, extending the flat of his hand to the big riverman.

"I thought this was bungholes and elbows?" Blanchard said with a disappointed tone. "Ain't no beer breaks in bungholes and elbows where I hail from."

"Just . . . hold up . . . a second," Clint said, breathing heavily. He eyed Blanchard. "You . . . take back that palaver . . . about my sainted mother . . . and I'll talk to the straw boss here."

"Your mother was never a part of it, lad, goat or saint. She may be the Mother Mary herse'f, for all this riverman knows." Blanchard laughed heartily, then his look grew serious and for the first time his tone rang with sincerity. "Work is all we want."

Clint turned to Sancho. "Let's back up here a minute."

Blanchard put his hands on his hips again, looking a bit disgusted with the time-out, but wanting the work more than the fight.

"Are you *sure* you don't need another crew?" Clint asked Sancho. A wry grin crossed Clint's face, then he winced with his split lip.

"We ain't et in two days," Blanchard put in, sheepish for the first time.

Sancho's gaze cut from Clint to Boulders, then back again. "Payday is Saturday at sundown," he said, rubbing a knot on the side of his head.

"Suits us," Blanchard said, then guffawed.

Sancho, limping, turned, went to his horse, and mounted. He reined over to where Blanchard's men were gathering around the big riverman.

"Blanchard!" Sancho snapped, but his

tone lost some of its effect since he was still breathing hard. The big riverman looked up from mopping the blood away with a kerchief. "I am *jefe* of this outfit and I will allow no back talk." Sancho rested his hand on the butt of the Allen's Pepperbox he carried shoved into his belt. "You do your work, work your men, and I will not have to shoot your boulders into pee gravel."

"Hell, man, I don't know what a *jefe* is, but I'll be proud to pull my wages and you'll be proud to pay 'em, an' I'll whip any man who don't pull his weight and a mite extra."

"That is good," Sancho said, "but let me assure you, amigo, you call me or any of these men greasers again. and you will be crawdad bait. The next fight will be from twenty paces." He tapped the Allen's with a bean-brown linger and reined away.

Blanchard merely grinned.

Clint regained his hat and mounted the palomino. He squared the hat on his head, then tipped it to Blanchard as he spun the horse.

"You hit right hard for a cowherd," Blanchard said mopping at his split brow.

"Don't let the duds an' horse fool you, Blanchard. A dozen years on holystoned decks and in the yardarms, and mine was the blue-water kind."

"Well, yer not near what you might be had you spent it on the river. But still, you ain't bad. I'll look forward to finishing that up sometimes when work don't beckon."

"Yeah, me too," Clint said with bravado. then spurted the palomino to catch up with Sancho, who crested the rise ahead, seemingly more than happy to be returning to the hacienda.

Clint's head throbbed like it had been used by the farrier to shape horseshoes, and every muscle in his body screamed with pain when the big horse pounded to catch up with the *segundo* of Rancho del Rio Ancho. Yeah, he was real anxious to square away with Boulders Blanchard again. About as anxious as he was to get in between the bull and the bear at one of Don Carlos Vega's rodeos.

Clint reined the palomino up beside Sancho's red roan. "I never did get around to asking what building that wood yard was all about?"

"Don Carlos has entered into a proposition with a new steamboat company."

"That pier you're building is quite an expense." Clint knew that Don Carlos, like most of California's dons, was long on land and cattle and painfully short on gold.

"The don was advanced money by Señor Hutchinson of the San Francisco-Benicia-Sacramento Steam Navigation Company. He will repay in wood, which we are gathering from all over the rancho. It will be good to clear the land, and get paid for it."

That made sense to Clint. Maybe the old don's money troubles were over.

They rode in silence for the next hour, each man nursing his wounds and keeping his own counsel.

After reining into a lane between vineyards, they made their way to the whitewashed buildings of the Rancho del Rio Ancho complex ahead, a shining white oasis standing amid lush green through a stand of live oaks. It had not changed since Clint had been here almost a year before.

A walled complex enclosed the main adobe hacienda with its red clay tile roof—each tile formed over the thigh of the maker—with the much smaller *cocina*—kitchen—building to the rear, and the smokehouse beyond it. Sycamores, ashes, cottonwoods, and live oaks surrounded and cooled the enclosure. A flight of turkeys rose into a sycamore as the dogs began their greeting clamor, and several chickens scattered.

Within the walls also lay a vegetable garden, now lush with squash, beans, pumpkins, melons, peppers of five varieties, and two dozen heavily laden fruit trees. Just outside the walls began the corrals, and in the center of that oak-and-pine-pole complex, stood the long, low *establo*—barn—and much smaller *matanza*—slaughterhouse.

Even in the heat, wispy plumes rose from the smokehouse and, of much greater interest to Clint, from the *cocina.* He had not eaten for a day and a half.

A pack of dogs met them at the entrance, a large twelve-foot opening in the adobe wall where two two-foot-diameter oak timbers supported a header bearing the rancho brand—a pair of serpentine lines representing the wide river itself—burned into each end of the fifteen-foot-long log, and the hand-carved letters *bienvenido*—welcome. Clinging, climbing bougainvillea, now bright with purple blooms, had been trimmed away so the letters and brands showed.

Don Carlos Vega opened the big carved door of the main house. He was easily recognizable with his shock of white hair contrasting against his dark windburned and lined face.

"El Lazo, you have arrived in time for the afternoon meal," he yelled in Spanish. "Join us, Sancho, after the horses are cared for."

Clint doffed his hat and dismounted. Though his gut felt as if it had dried to his backbone, as much as he wanted to eat, he wanted even more to hear why the don had asked him to come from so far down the valley. It had been more than a hundred-mile, four-day ride. He shook hands with the man while Sancho led the horses away.

"A meal I could use. But you didn't invite me here to feed me," Clint said in the language of his host.

"There is time enough for an old man's troubles, amigo, after we eat." He clamped a hand on Clint's shoulder. "Apolonia ran to her room when she saw your approach. Her simple homespun frock was obviously not elegant enough for your visit. You know women!" He moved toward the house. "Now I will pour you a glass of vino and you will tell me of your horses and how your trip south was. But first, why do you and my *segundo* look as if you've tangled with an old *oso?*"

58

"No bear, Don Carlos, just a bear of a man who had a strange way of applying for a job. It's a resolved matter now."

"Good."

Clint followed the old man through the wide *zaguán,* entry, of the house, and into its great room. The old don spoke quietly to an Indian woman who hurried away for the wine. He fetched a cedar humidor from the mantel over a fireplace big enough to step into and offered a cigar to Clint, who, out of politeness, accepted.

They sat in tall straight-backed leather chairs in front of the vacant hearth and lit up before either spoke. Clint was asked about the horses, a fine herd of forty Andalusians he had selected from Rancho del Rio Ancho stock as payment for recovering the don's daughter, Apolonia. She had been kidnapped by a sea captain who made a business of trading in human flesh, the devil's bounty.

Clint described the trip south and the piece of land he had selected for his own ranch—a site far down the central valley where few white men had been, stretching south from the Kaweah River to the Tule. A piece of land he had spent many days negotiating with a Yocuts chief to buy. But as

59

he spoke he detected an uncharacteristic nervousness in the don—not a passing thing, but a deep gnawing worm in the older man's gut.

He hoped somehow this trip might solve his own problem—money— as well as the old don's. The old chief had wanted some of Clint's stock, but for his tribe to eat, not ride. For this price they had agreed to live together in peace on the land, with Clint to raise horses and cattle, and the Yocuts to hunt and fish and gather as they always had. Clint needed money to buy the two dozen head of horses—crowbaits would do as well as fine Andalusians—to drive back to the chief to seal their bargain. He had tried to convince the Yocuts to accept cattle or to let him and Gideon hunt deer and elk for the tribe, but only horses would do.

Clint's newest problem was both that and a blessing. The gold rush had driven the price of horses from five dollars to fifty a head since Clint had ridden south. He was shocked when he stopped at the little settlement of Stockton—named after his old boss—and tried to negotiate for some swaybacked nags he saw in the livery there. And if he did not get back to the ranch soon, his friend Gideon might have one hell of a time keeping the herd together, and keeping the Yocuts from putting a few of the valuable Andalusian's into their boiling baskets.

Clint glanced up to see Apolonia Vega enter the room with a swish of scarlet lace and a swirl of long black hair.

He rose and extended his right hand, which she took warmly with her left. Then, to his surprise, she moved forward and, on her tiptoes, slid an arm around his neck and placed her warm cheek against his for a moment. She brushed his cheek with her lips.

Apolonia backed away with a smile and sparkling ebony eyes that warmed the room even more than the powerful valley sun outside had already done.

Noting his surprise, she laughed gaily. "If a girl cannot be familiar with the man who saved her life—and more—then with whom may she be familiar?" Apolonia asked, suddenly serious. She glanced at her father, whose silence seemed approval enough.

Clint laughed and pulled a chair over for Apolonia. "For whatever reason, I'm pleased to be so warmly greeted by the most beautiful woman in California," he managed, but his cheek remained hot with embarrassment at the girl's greeting—particularly in front of her father. And the heat in Clint's loins caused him even more discomfort.

The don's indulgent smile betrayed only pleasure.

The Indian woman returned to the room and served the men a goblet of rich red wine and Apolonia a cup of tea.

The don offered his drink in toast. "To the new Alta California . . . may all her residents, new and old, live in peace, harmony, and fairness."

"I'll drink to that, *saludo*," Clint said, clicking his goblet against Don Carlos's, then Apolonia's teacup. "And to prosperity . . . and beauty." His eyes locked with hers for a fleeting moment. As they drank Sancho entered and also pulled up a chair.

"We men are now going to talk business, *querida*," the don said, using a term of endearment and reaching over to pat his daughter on the knee. Apolonia rose, and Clint did also as she left the room. Obviously, the don had changed his mind and was unwilling to wait until after dinner to vent his apparent frustrations.

"Join us again at supper, my dear," Don Carlos called after her.

Clint's eyes followed her until she disappeared out into the hacienda's central courtyard.

"What can I do to be of service?" Clint asked, turning his attention back to the white-haired don, anxious to get to the point, but not so eager to get back to his budding ranch now that he was reminded of how beautiful Apolonia Vega was, and how sweet and clean she smelled. The odor of lilac lingered on his cheek and hands, and distracted him as Don Carlos rose and began to pace.

"I have a small problem you might be of help with." the don said. He waved at the Indian woman who stood near the door, indicating he wanted more wine. Then he continued. "I have contracted with a Senor Garth Hutchinson of the San Francisco-Benicia-Sacramento Steam Navigation Company to supply firewood for their boilers. He promised to advance money on a weekly basis, at least a week in advance, to make payroll while we construct a landing and stockpile wood, but he is late with his third payment . . . and I have a payroll due in three days, Saturday."

Clint smiled inwardly as he traded glances with Sancho, who remained silent.

If Saturday night rolled around and they could not pay ol' Boulders Blanchard and his rivermen, the first fight at the river might seem a Sunday picnic.

"But that is small compared to a problem facing all the old families," the don continued, his manner cold and concise. "The new governor of California has called together a group of men from all over the state to serve as the California Land Commission. These men are meeting in Monterey to determine the fate of all those who owned land in California at the time of her great revolution and acquisition by the *Estados Unidos.*"

He paused as the Indian woman appeared with a carafe of wine and refilled their goblets.

"Is this bad?" Clint asked innocently. "I know that Governor Pico madly issued a number of grants right before the revolution to many of his friends and to those he owed favors, and that didn't set well with the *Americanos.*"

The old don reddened. "That is one thing, and is neither here nor there, Lazo. They are also judging the validity of the ownership of lands that have been in families for generations . . . my own rancho for instance." The don walked to a shuttered window, flung it open, and pointed to a low knoll in the distance and a small fenced and well-tended plot.

"On that rise lay three generations of Vegas. My grandfather came here from Mexico in 1772, and for his service to the King of Spain was granted these twelve square leagues of land. Land that was mostly swamp and undergrowth. Land that bore no cattle or horses or vineyards or . . ." He seemed to choke up, but turned away from the window and his misted eyes lit with fire.

"They must not doubt the title of this rancho, Lazo, or we must rise up against them . . . and I do not wish this to happen." He crossed back to his seat and collapsed into it, his proud manner gone. He seemed to collapse like a wine bladder pouring out its contents into the sand. He coughed, drank deeply from the goblet, then motioned to the old woman again.

Clint cleared his throat before he spoke. "Why do you question the outcome of this California Land Commission hearing? Certainly they are fair—"

"Fair! If this commission was fair, it would be filled by men who had been here in California for generations, by men who knew first hand her families and how they have cared for the land since that time."

"And it's not served by Californios?" Clint asked.

"No! No Californios were selected. It is served only by Anglos, by newcomers, by men who know nothing of the history of this land."

Clint remained silent for a moment, digesting what he'd been told. He sipped his own wine before he spoke. "Surely there are records—"

"In 1820 there was a great fire in Monterey. The government building and all records were destroyed." The don's shoulders sagged even more. "Shortly afterward, the governor suggested we refile, but these ranchos had been in families for years, their borders and boundaries well established by custom. Few took the trouble to refile . . . and my father was one of the many who did not."

"Still, I must believe that these men are basically fair and—"

"Fair? Do you think it is fair for Californios who were born in this great land to have to pay a foreigner's tax of thirty dollars, a great tax for some poor *paisanos,* to be able to mine her mountains, when Anglos arrive daily and bear no such burden for the same privilege? This you consider the act of fair men? And this is only one of many acts that illustrate their 'fairness.'

"Point well taken, Don Carlos." Clint sighed deeply and finished off his wine. To tax the Mexicans who had been here for two hundred years with a foreign miner's tax was a bit absurd. "What can I do to be of service?"

"You know personally many of those who serve on the commission. Señors Edward Fitzgerald Beale and John Charles Frémont and many more are in attendance. Go there, and be our advocate."

"I'm no lawyer."

"I know that, but you speak both languages, and you have proven your loyalty to my family and your abilities to me. You are the only Anglo I can trust with this matter. You will carry a letter with my seal authorizing you to act in our stead."

"How long do you expect this to take?"

"It could be months," the old don said, then, anticipating Clint's concern, promised, "I will send two vaqueros to the Kaweah to join your associate, Gideon."

67

"We need horses to complete our bargain with the Yocuts to gain the right to use the land."

"How many horses?" Sancho spoke for the first time since he entered the room. The horses on the ranch were his responsibility and his pride.

"Two dozen, but they can be the worst of the lot. All they have to do is be able to make the drive south. As you know, the Yocuts keep them for meat, not service."

"Done," Don Carlos said without consulting Sancho, who cast a hard glance at his *patrón*.

"There are many mustangs running wild in the canyons between here and Napa," Sancho said quickly, fearing for the stock he had spent so many years developing. "I see no reason to use Rio Ancho Andalusians, no matter how poor some might be."

"Anything on four feet that will make the drive," Clint consoled the vaquero, "but it must be soon."

"I will ride in the morning with six men, if that meets with your approval, *jefe*. Old man Pope has invited us to come into his valley and the surrounding hills to take horses. They destroy his crops."

"Done."

"And you'll be on the trail in a fortnight?" Clint asked, still concerned.

"My word," Sancho offered, extending his hand.

"Two dozen wild mustangs is too little payment for saving this rancho," Don Carlos said.

"What more do you suggest?" Clint asked, knowing the old don to always be more than fair.

"I am not a man of commerce, Lazo. This wood yard was agreed to only as a means to get my land cleared. It seems to me that farming is the future of Rio Ancho, and one must have clear land to farm. I have no interest in it otherwise. It is a dirty business with men I dislike. You secure good and rightful title to Rancho del Rio Ancho from these Anglos in Monterey, and I will lease you the five acres on the river, assign you my agreement with the steamship company, and give you the right to clear my rancho for the wood."

"How much for the lease?" Clint asked, suddenly more than merely interested. He would have helped the old don for nothing, but this could be a boon that would finance his own ranch.

"For so long as you own the business, for

one dollar per year. We will retain the right to use the pier for our own purposes when necessary, which should not be often. If you sell it, then we will decide on a fair lease price that meets the market for the new owner."

"That's not fair to you—"

"It is a small piece of land, we have two leagues along the river, more than six of your Anglo miles, and you have been a good friend. And I need all the Anglo friends I can get, it seems."

Clint rose and shook hands with the don. "It sounds more than fair to me, Don Carlos. Do you have a written agreement with this Hutchinson?"

"I will fetch it to your room. Now you go and rest and I will have the women bring water. You can read it at your leisure while the *cocino* prepares our supper."

"Perhaps a piece of fruit in the meantime?" Clint asked, suddenly starving.

"I am sorry, Lazo. I have been rude and concerned only with my own problems."

"I understand," Clint said with compassion. A group of men unknown to the old don, men foreign to him, were debating his and his family's future at a place far away in a language he did not understand.

And their ruling would be the law of the land.

As Clint followed the Indian woman to the guest room, he was both concerned and elated. This could solve all his problems. But then again . . . He had selected the piece of land far down the valley, far from the seat of government of the new state, far from men who might know of the warrant for his arrest that might still be outstanding. To go to Monterey would be to place himself among them again.

Still, it was an opportunity to be of service to Don Carlos—and to Apolonia—that he could not pass by, no matter what the risk.

Tomorrow he would ride for Benicia and catch a boat to San Francisco, see this Hutchinson, and get the don's advance money—now a self-serving errand, as the woodyard was to be his—then go on to Monterey and verify that Rancho del Rio Ancho was not at risk.

In a few days, he hoped no more, he would be well on his way to being able to build the finest horse ranch in California.

Or in a Monterey *jusgado*—what the gringos were calling a hoosegow.

It was a risk well worth taking.

4

It was not that Big Henry Slocumb was so physically large, just that he acted that way. He was of average height, though thick of neck, chest, back, thighs, and biceps. His hair was big, its rust-red mass curled out over his ears and hung to the middle of his neck, and his beard had been big before he had to shave it, a result of it being singed to a black mess in the wreck of the *Queen Anne*. His hair surrounded his face and broad features like a Christmas wreath. Most of his life he had backed up his nickname, Big Henry, with bluster, and he made enough money that his bank account made him just a little larger in most men's eyes.

He did not really need a job. He had saved a little of what he had made piloting the *Queen Anne* up and down the Sacramento for better than five months, and a little from what he had made piloting the many riverboats before her on the Mississippi watershed. But he was determined to have a job nevertheless, for it was the only way to prove he was the stud duck on the river, and to better his archenemy, Ezekiel Hammond. Ever since Hammond forced the *Queen* onto Point Chapman and destroyed her, and cost Big Henry most of her freight and twenty-six men—and most importantly, his reputation—Slocumb could not get Hammond out of his mind.

Besides, it was rumored Hammond was being paid $ 1,750 per month by the California Steam Navigation Company. That alone was enough to gall Slocumb, for Big Henry knew he was a better man, and no man was a better pilot. Hell, didn't he have the record from Natchez to New Orleans. He still claimed it, even though another pilot and boat had since lied about their time in bettering it. At least Henry knew in his heart that they lied.

Yes, he wanted a job, and now, standing on long Wharf eyeing the *Benicia Belle* while he lit up his cigar, he decided that this was just the boat he needed to prove his point to the world. Now, if half what he had heard about her in the saloons of San Francisco was true . . .

"You Henry Slocumb?"

Big Henry turned and glowered at the dark-haired man in the fancy cutaway coat who had spoken. Henry was farsighted, but it did not affect his ability to operate his boats. He could see plain enough beyond twenty feet, and it was a lot farther than that from the water to the glassed-in pilot-house where he ruled the river in any of the boats he would deign to operate.

"Who wants to know?" Henry snarled, and chomped down on the long nine he smoked.

"I'm Garth Hutchinson, owner and master of the *Benicia Belle,* and I'm the man who sent for you."

"Owner maybe, but if 'n I sign on, she'll have only one master."

"*If* you're signed on, we'll see about that. You didn't do too well for the *Queen Anne.*"

For a minute Garth thought the man was going to walk away, that his ears would redden until they burst into flame, then he seemed to reconsider, chomped down on his cigar, and turned back to study the boat. He folded his hands behind him and rocked back on his heels.

Garth Hutchinson surveyed the shorter but thicker man, trying to determine if his

74

bulk was muscle or suet and could not make up his mind. Instead, he turned his attention back to the business at hand—he could not operate on the river without a pilot, and pilots were scarce as honest politicians, at least in California.

His tone softened. "Let's go aboard. We'll talk details after you look her over."

"I've never turned down a chance to look a boat over, but that don't mean ya'll got yourself a pilot."

"Let's go aboard." Garth led the way without checking to see if Slocumb followed.

He shuffled back and forth a moment, scratched his head through his mass of curly red hair, chomped even harder on the long nine, furrowed his brow, then finally hurried after.

After Hutchinson had taken him from stem to stern and bilge to pilothouse, each stood with one hand on her eight-foot-diameter wheel, the bottom half of which extended through the deck into the space below, and the other hand clutching a shot glass of whiskey Garth had poured them. He finished his sales pitch.

"She's sure to be the fastest and most maneuverable boat on the river." He waited for Slocumb to speak.

The man had remained almost silent as Garth had shown him around—a fact Garth considered a good sign. He had found nothing to bluster or pop off about.

"She seems a proper enough boat," Slocumb said with unusual candor. "Now, if your proposition is the best on the river, we can get to making her pay."

"A thousand a month—"

"Two thousand, or we've got nothing to talk about."

"Then we've got nothing to talk about. I hope you enjoyed the tour." Garth drained his shot glass. He turned away and studied the bay, its flotilla of empty ships, and Alcatraz and Angel Island beyond. "I'm a little busy, Mr. Slocumb, so if you'll excuse me . . ."

Henry Slocumb tried to think of something to say, but remained dumbfounded. No one talked to river pilots, pilots who carried proper papers as issued by the United States Congress, that way. Didn't this man know who and what the hell Big Henry Slocumb was?

"I got things to do myself," Henry said, his face beginning to redden.

"Good day," Garth said mildly, without looking over his shoulder or paying the least attention to whether or not Slocumb was leaving.

Henry shuffled back and forth, finished his whiskey, then reached into his waistcoat pocket for another cigar. He lit up, and Hutchinson still had not turned from staring out the big glass enclosure.

"I don't need no job, you know?" Henry mumbled, still getting no answer from Hutchinson. Slocumb took a long drag on the cigar, exhaled slowly, coughed, then asked quietly, "Just how much did you have in mind again?"

"One thousand a month."

"That's chicken feed," Slocumb said, beginning to heat up like the *Belle*'s boilers. "A man couldn't hold 'is head up—"

"That's five times what I've ever paid a man—"

"Then you've never hired an able pilot . . . and that's not the going rate on the river. You lose a boat and you'll wish you had paid a good man a fair wage."

"Like you lost the *Queen Anne?*" For a moment Garth thought Slocumb was going to leap the distance between them, then his ears began to fade again.

He spoke with the cigar clamped between his teeth. "I had the bloody right of way into Som'bitch Slough. Ezekiel Hammond is the worst bilge on the river."

"Nevertheless, you lost the Queen Anne, and Ezekiel Hammond is the only one of the five pilots on the river making more than a thousand a month. I've checked."

Slocumb chose to ignore this. "He ran me aground with a boat of almost twice the tonnage."

"The way I heard it, you closed on a small channel against a boat of almost twice the tonnage, lost your boat and cargo, and twenty-six men died. A foolish act, no matter who had the right-of-way."

"Unlucky, maybe," Slocumb said sheepishly.

"A thousand a month against two percent of the gross. We take in a hundred thousand a month and you've got your two thousand. That's my last offer."

Slocumb studied Hutchinson a moment, weighing what he had proposed. "What do you figure on grossing? Fifty thousand, right?"

"If we don't do a hell of a lot better than that, I'll be damned unhappy. You stand to make more than Ezekiel Hammond . . . maybe a lot more."

Slocumb grinned and extended his hand.

"Before we seal this bargain with a handshake, there's something you'd better know." Hutchinson did not return Slocumb's grin, but rather looked as hard and cold as the brass hub on the boat's huge wheel.

"What's that?" Slocumb asked, his brow furrowed and his hand dropping.

"You get 'unlucky' with the *Belle* like you did with the Queen, and I'll kill you." Hutchinson's tone rang cold as the bay and twice as flat. There was no question he meant exactly what he said.

Slocumb's jaw clamped and the two men locked stares. Big Henry Slocumb had never been talked to that way. Finally his eyes drifted away to the side, then the door behind him opened, and he turned to face the most beautiful woman he'd ever seen; her emerald eyes melted any doubts he might have had.

"Are you the new pilot?" Rachel DuBois asked. her voice ringing like a bell and her smile promising things Henry Slocumb had only dreamed about with women of half her looks.

"Henry Slocumb," he said as he snatched his narrow-billed pilot's hat off his head. "The finest river pilot ever to dodge a snag."

"Rachel DuBois, the *Belle*'s singer and official hostess," she said. "Welcome aboard. I've heard it said there is no one better with a riverboat, Mr. Slocumb. You'll be entrusted with my safety, and all of our passengers, and I'm pleased." She extended her hand just as a man might. The warmth of it seared him. "I hope you gentlemen can join me in the salon for dinner." She spun on her heel and, with the rustle of silk and the odor of lilac, disappeared as quickly as she'd appeared. Henry took a moment to catch his breath before he turned back to Hutchinson.

"She'll be a lucky boat," Slocumb said quietly. "And she'll do more than a hundred thousand a month, 'cause I'm gonna make more than Ezekiel Hammond ever dreamed of."

"I'm master, you're the pilot," Garth said, his hard look not wavering. "I'll not tell you how or where to run the boat, operationally speaking, and you'll stay out of the cargo handling and the rest of her business."

"Done." Slocumb extended his hand again, still warm from Rachel's touch, and was surprised at Hutchinson's steel grip. His own was molded iron from years at the massive wheels.

And he was even more surprised that his new boss made no mention of him staying away from Rachel DuBois.

One thing Big Henry Slocumb knew for sure—women couldn't resist a river pilot.

Clint reined up and looked down at the little town of Benicia with its back bay and inlet off the Sacramento. He had hoped to catch one of the larger boats at the landing, but was disappointed to note nothing but scows, flatboats, and mackinaws. He shaded his eyes and searched the river behind him, and then the water leading on down to Carquinez Straights and the bay. No big boats in sight. He'd have to make do. He touched the spurs to Diablo, and the big horse broke into a lope down the hill. He didn't slow until he reined up at the landing.

One of the flatboats moored there carried a pair of masts, ketch-rigged, and though a hermaphrodite—half keelboat, half sail —seemed a little better designed than the others. He dismounted and made his way along the pile of rocks that served as quay until he was even with her. A single man worked on her deck.

"Ahoy, the boat!" Clint shouted, and was surprised to see the same scarecrow preacher who had confronted him on the river turn and wave. His thin face broke into a smile and he stepped into the catboat tied alongside and pulled oar the thirty feet to the quay.

He climbed out of the boat and extended his bony hand. "I'm Moses McClanahan. Don't believe we traded names the last time we met."

Clint shook with the man. "Clint Ryan. You give up your piece of the shore?"

"Nope. Gonna build a permanent church there to pass the gospel along to the heathen . . . an' they're thicker than sardines on this river, don't ya know. Church of the River Redeemer. But sinners are sure enough everywhere, and particularly in San Francisco. Headed there now to save a few . . . an' arrange for some building materials, don't ya know."

"I'm hunting a lift there. Don't suppose a preacher would trade a ride for a good hand with those sails?"

"You bet. Of course, a body would want to put a few coins, say a half-dollar's worth, in the offerin' to help with the Lord's work if'n he catched a ride, work or not, on the Lord's boat . . . and I'm not only a preacher, but a prophet."

"For a dollar a man could ride a fine riverboat—" Clint started to complain.

"Those boats be the work of the devil with gamblin' and women, don't ya know. An' besides, a body would have to wait until day after tomorrow to catch a riverboat. Last one to San Francisco just left not more than an hour ago. Cost more'n a half-dollar and a pound of flesh to stay here and get et by bedbugs, don't ya know." He slapped the back of his neck. "Not to speak of these hummingbird-sized skeeters."

Clint smiled and shook his head in rather disgusted surrender, then added sarcastically, "God knows I'd hate to be exposed to a woman, and I'd love to put a few coins in the pot to do His work." *And I've got to get to this Hutchinson in time to get Don Carlos Vega's advance money and get those crazy rivermen paid if I don't want a war to start.*

"Then climb aboard." Moses smiled broadly.

"Can we get her in a little closer? I've got to get this animal aboard."

"That's another half-dollar." Moses's smile faded.

"For a dollar, Mr. McClanahan, you ought to part the water and let Diablo walk aboard."

"Don't blaspheme . . . and you can drop the mister, don't ya know. It's Prophet or just plain Moses, if ya'll prefer. Come on and help me pole her in a little closer."

Clint climbed aboard the catboat, still shaking his head. They got the strange blunt-ended boat in close enough so that Diablo could climb aboard and within fifteen minutes had caught the current of the outgoing tide as well as the river's flow, had main sail and mizzen flying, and were well on their way at better than twelve knots.

The feeling of halyards and running rigging was good in Clint's hands again, and even though the boat was a slug in the water, he was enjoying himself. It was close to midnight by the time they snaked their way through the bay's currents and quirks to reach San Francisco, and were lucky at that, for the tide was beginning to turn.

A dollar lighter, Clint parted ways with the wild-eyed preached Moses McClanahan, having to swim Diablo part of the way ashore until the big horse found footing in the mud. Moses would not bring his boat, named the *Lord's Work,* close to the unfamiliar shore, and certainly would not pay the dollar the Long Wharf or any of the others would require to tie up alongside.

Soaking wet, Clint and Diablo had no more than reached the shore when a thick fog rolled in. For the first time in three months, Clint trembled, cold to the bone. They worked along the waterfront until they found Long Wharf and the offices of the San Francisco-Benicia-Sacramento Steam Navigation Company, but it and the *Benicia Belle* lay dark except for the *Belle's* anchor light. Clint decided he would get nothing done this night, so at a trot they made their way into town where he located a livery.

Clint found himself stuck for another half-dollar, but the hostler kindly consented to his sleeping in the same stall as Diablo for no extra charge, and gave the big horse a forkful of hay and the luxury of a pint of oats.

And Clint did try to sleep, but directly behind the livery, facing the other way, the noise and tinkling music of a saloon continued to tease him. Finally he crawled out of his bedroll and made his way across the alley to find the rear door of the place. Sodden, straw in his hair from the stall, and a bit less than presentable, he shouldered his way through a crowd of miners and townsmen to the bar—and decided to spend his fourth half-dollar of the day, even though it was a luxury he could ill afford. Shouting over the din, he ordered a glass of the house swill.

He no more than touched the glass of whiskey to his mouth when the glass exploded into a thousand shards.

Instinctively, Clint hit the floor, palming his Colt's, the shot ringing in his ears. He immediately realized that he was not the target, for the gunman, gray-headed and rawboned, was panning his Walker away from Clint. Others scrambled out of the way, leaving Clint crouched next to the bar, the gunman a half-dozen paces away, and another man standing near Clint, at little more than an arm's length.

Every other man in the place remained silent, not wanting to attract the gunman's attention.

The gunman snarled with resolve, and his gray eyes, deep and dark-rimmed, narrowed as the saloon grew deathly quiet.

"Ain't no Ethiopian gonna lay hands on me," the man spat. He seemed a bit unsteady, Clint thought as he studied the man. Like he'd been leaning on the bar far too long.

Clint glanced at the man standing close

to him and realized that he was black and big, and his eyes sparked with fire—but he was unarmed. The gunman had the heavy Walker extended at arm's length and pointed dead center at the big black's chest.

Clint, his own Colt's cocked and leveled at the shooter, slowly rose to his feet, speaking in a level, related tone. "I don't know what this is all about, but outside would be a better place—"

"You stay out of this!" the gunman snapped, keeping his big-bored Walker Colt's leveled on the other man.

Clint wiped his mouth with the back of his free hand and it came away covered with blood from the shards of the glass. He said quietly, "You put me in it, friend."

"Well, get out of it . . . now. This man laid hands on me, and he's a-gonna die."

Another man stepped out of the crowd, well dressed with a high hat, a swallowtail coat, and pleated waistcoat, his fancy silver-handled walking stick pointed at the gunman—but only as if to make a point. "My name is Garth Hutchinson. You spoke out of turn, friend"—he addressed the man with the Walker—"when you made a remark about Miss DuBois. Joshua here is my man, and is obliged to watch over her. Miss DuBois was never employed in New Orleans, particularly in the kind of establishment you suggested."

"I don't give a damn who you are, fancy man, or what you think. I know what I know." The gray-headed gunman glowered at Hutchinson—who, Clint realized, was the same man he was searching for. "I'm gonna blow 'your man' here into his reward."

"Just put the pistol down and walk out of here." Clint warned evenly. The man turned his attention back to Clint, unsteadily swinging the Walker his way.

Instinctively, before the bore could come to bear on him, Clint fired.

The big Walker sailed aside as Clint's .44-caliber bullet took the man in his gun-arm shoulder and blew him spinning backward.

The crowded barroom gave a few more steps back.

Stumbling as if he was about to go down, the shooter grimaced, recovered his footing, and grasped his right shoulder with his left hand, the blood seeping through his fingertips.

"Don't shoot me again," he pleaded, fear

in his eyes. Clint moved the muzzle of the Colt's just enough so it was no longer centered on the man. The gray-headed man regained some confidence, and arrogance. "That was cold, mister," he snarled, gasping.

"Not as cold as I'd have been if I'd let you come down on me with that blunderbuss."

Clint still had his Navy Colt's leveled near the shooter when the batwing doors behind him burst open and two men charged in—both wearing stars on their chests.

"Drop that," one demanded, bringing a sawed-off shotgun to bear on Clint.

"Easy with that scattergun," Clint said, and lowered the Colt's to his side.

"I said drop it." The other man also had a cut-down rifle, both men armed for close work.

"It's cocked, now just stand easy while I let the hammer down. I'd hate to blow somebody's toe off by accident."

"Ease it down," the deputy said. "Then drop it."

Clint ratcheted the hammer down, then let the Colt's fall to the floor.

"Hands on the bar," the deputy ordered,

and Clint complied. Then the deputy turned his attention to the barman, who was tentatively rising from where he had hidden behind the bar. "What happened here?"

"The black there and the fellow bleedin' traded words and the bleedin' one drew down on him. I thought it was all over till this one"—he pointed at Clint—"just shot him like a dog."

"How the hell would you know?" Clint snapped. "You were lower than a snake's belly behind the bar."

"This man's right. That's not the way it was." Garth Hutchinson stepped forward, next to Clint.

"And who are you?" the deputy asked.

"Garth Hutchinson, president of the San Francisco-Benicia-Sacramento Steam Navigation Company."

"We're taking these fellows in, Hutchinson. This one's going to the doc's." He motioned to the wounded man to go outside, which he did with a stagger. "If you got something to say, I'd suggest you come to the city marshal's office and tell it to the boss."

One of the deputies moved forward and pushed Clint away from his Colt's, then reached down and gathered it up and stuck it into his belt.

"All I did was keep from being shot . . . self-defense," Clint said, his voice a little strained for the first time.

"That's the way 'twas." The big black tried to defend Clint.

"You keep your black mouth shut," the deputy growled. "Both of you get outside before you have to be carried there."

As they moved to the batwing doors Joshua turned to Clint. "I 'preciate what ya'll did."

"No problem," Clint said, then was pushed violently from behind, as was Joshua.

"I said to keep your mouths shut," the deputy snarled.

"Don't worry, I'll be along to get you out, Joshua," Garth Hutchinson called from behind.

Clint turned back to tell Hutchinson what his mission was, but the deputy shoved him violently out across the plank walkway into the road. Clint looked at the armed man like a bull at a bastard calf, but wisely said nothing.

That's great, just great, Clint thought. I find the man I've come to find and can't say a word to him.

They piled Clint and Joshua in the back of a closed-in wagon, along with two fellas who lay sprawled in their own vomit, and shut and locked the doors behind them. It was dark as a foot up a bull's backside when the doors closed, and smelled even worse. In a moment the team was whipped up and the wagon bouncing along. But not to jail, as Clint surmised. The wagon made four more stops, and as many more men, most dead drunk with its resulting stench, were thrown in the back before an hour passed and they arrived.

They all piled out into a muddy alley behind a two-story barred-windowed brick building and, to the prodding of rifles and billy clubs, made their way inside.

With the disdain of a man who had performed the same act ten thousand times, a guard took their names and noted them on a piece of paper. Clint and Joshua were shoved into a single cell and took the top two bunks—only eighteen inches wide and laced with hemp rope. Each man barely fit. The bunks and floor below were soon loaded with drunks.

"Again, I 'preciate what ya'll did," Joshua said in the darkness.

"It was mostly to protect my own hide, friend, not yours. Save your thanks."

"Still and all, he woulda shot me."

"Still might. You and I both. I probably should have blown his mule-gray head off instead of holing his gun arm. They wouldn't of thrown me any deeper into jail if I had."

Joshua chuckled for the first time.

With the stench of vomit in his nostrils and a knot of disgust in his chest, Clint managed to fall asleep.

He awoke to find two deputies pulling Joshua out of the cell. "You're being released," one man said.

"Joshua," Clint called after him, trying to clear his head from the hard sleep he had fallen into. "I'm Clint Ryan. I came here to talk with your boss. Get him to bail me out, too."

"I'll ask," Joshua managed to call back, before he was jabbed with a billy.

"Shut your black mouth or I'll put you right back in there."

"I have to talk to him!" Clint shouted.

"Shut up!" rang down the hall, and was repeated by a dozen half-asleep men in the cells alongside.

Damn, I should've talked with him last night, Clint chided himself. *It might be days before they get around to a hearing, and I've only got two to get that payroll back to Don Carlos—and Boulders Blanchard and his rivermen.*

It was an hour before the guards came back carrying a bucket of slop they called breakfast and two dozen tin cups to dip in it.

"I've got to get a message to Garth Hutchinson!" Clint shouted down the hallway to the guards who were passing out the gruel.

They ignored him until they reached his cell. "I've got to get—"

"And I've got to get one to the Emperor of China," the guard snapped. "If you want to eat and get out of here for a piss break, you'll keep your trap shut. Otherwise I'll let you piss your pants.

Clint fought the urge to reach through the bars and throttle the man, but he did need to relieve himself. He took his cup of slop, smelled it, then gave it to a ruddy-faced man who looked as if he hadn't eaten in a month of Sundays and had already finished his own.

Resigned, Clint climbed up on his bunk and waited. It was late afternoon before a guard came and called his name.

94

"Ryan! You've got a visitor."

He was on his feet and waiting at the bars long before the guard reached the lock.

Clint was shown upstairs to the marshal's office.

He entered and a stout graying man in dark coat and cravat, sporting a large-brimmed white hat, brushed by him. Garth Hutchinson reclined on the edge of a desk and called out, "Thanks, Marshal," as the man in the hat closed the door behind him.

He turned his attention to Clint. "You told my man Joshua you had something to say to me? You've got five minutes."

"Did you bail me out?"

"You're accused of assault and attempted murder. Your bail is five hundred dollars." Hutchinson looked Clint up and down, and Clint felt self-conscious knowing he smelled of the jail and looked like hell. Hutchinson pulled a cigar out of his waist-coat pocket and lit up, not bothering to offer Clint one. He exhaled, trailing a plume of smoke.

"You don't look like a man who's worth five dollars, much less five hundred, Ryan. And you've used up a minute of your time."

"I represent Don Carlos Vega."

"As what?"

"As his representative," Clint growled, irritation beginning to overcome self-consciousness. "I've got a letter of authorization back at the liv—back where I'm staying. You owe him an advance on the woodyard project, and I've come to collect it."

"That's it?" Garth Hutchinson rose as if he was about to leave.

"I guess, except I need your assurance you're sending that money *today.* He's got a payroll day after tomorrow."

Hutchinson laughed. "And just what the hell are you or old Don Carlos going to do about it if I don't have the money there?"

Clint was in no position to threaten, and even though his neck was beginning to feel the glow of anger, he worked at keeping his tone mild. "That's not the point, Mr. Hutchinson. If you want wood to serve your riverboat, you'll get the payroll money there. There's plenty of work in California now, and those men will walk off the job in a heartbeat."

Hutchinson pondered a moment, then his tone turned serious. "Did you mean to shoot that loudmouth in the shoulder?"

"I normally hit what I aim at."

"Can you handle yourself with your hands?"

"As good as the next man, better than most."

"Where are you from? Ryan's your name?"

Normally Clint would have suggested that an inquisitive man mind his own business, but he decided he needed this man's goodwill . . . at least for a while. He gave Hutchinson a quick rundown on his past, leaving out the part about the warrant he feared was still outstanding for him. Hutchinson's attitude slowly changed, and finally he leaned forward, interested.

"Then if you served in the revolution, do you know Beale, Frémont, and Stockton?" Hutchinson asked, his eyes narrowed.

"Know them well, and most the others who served. I served with or under all of them during the revolution. Beale, Gillespie, and Frémont are friends, Stockton offered to help me in more than one way. I knew Kearny."

"Kearny died in Mexico City," Hutchinson grumbled, since the general could be no help to him. He considered this information for a moment, knowing it was very likely that Stockton would soon end up as governor of California, and Frémont had been elected senator and was one of California's most influential men. Ryan might just prove to he far more valuable than he appeared. And he had already proved to be good with a gun, and more important, very levelheaded.

Hutchinson walked behind the marshal's desk and peered out the tall thin window to the street below as he considered his options. One thing he liked was having a man in his debt, particularly a man who might do him some good, and if he got this one out of jail . . .

After a long draw on the cigar, he exhaled a billow of smoke and turned back. "I need a master-at-arms on board the *Belle*. I'll bail you out, but only if you take the job. I may also need you to introduce me to some of your old friends."

"Thanks, but I've got a job. After you give me the payroll and I get it back to Rancho del Rio Ancho, I've got to go to Monterey and make sure the don's property rights are protected. You use some of that payroll on my bail, and Don Carlos will pay you back."

Hutchinson chuckled quietly. "I don't know that, friend. And your problems may be a little difficult to solve from that jail cell below. But it's interesting to know that the Vegas title is at stake . . . hell, he soon may not own the land or the wood that I need."

Clint's jaw knotted. Getting out was the important thing. "The Vegas have owned that land for a hundred years, their title is assured. How long does this job of yours last?"

"A couple of months will do, until I can find a man as good with a gun . . . and as levelheaded as you demonstrated yourself to be. I hope that wasn't just a fluke—or fear?"

Clint ignored the question. "I'll have to have a few days to get to Monterey and back."

"You hire a couple of guards, get them trained, and before we make our maiden voyage up the river the end of next week, you can take a couple of days to visit Monterey. Pay's twenty dollars a week. You'll have another thirty to pay the two guards, split any way you want . . . and of course, you'll have to pay me back the bail money."

And that'll take a hell of a lot longer then two months. Hutchinson smiled tightly. *And maybe, just maybe, I can see that the Vegas' property title becomes even more seriously in question—and buy it real cheap from the old Mexican.*

Clint suddenly got a sour taste in his mouth, but he had little choice. Reluctantly, he extended his hand. Hutchinson shook, but kept a hard look.

"Don't let me down, Ryan. I don't take kindly to men who don't do their jobs. We'll be carrying a lot of rowdy men up the river, and a hell of a lot of gold back down. I've got a contract with I.C. Woods at Adam's Express, and I don't want to lose it."

"If I take a job on, it gets done, Hutchinson."

"It had better." His tone rang hard and his eyes burned into Clint's. The tall dark man nodded, then walked to the door and waved the guard in who had brought Clint up.

Hutchinson was back to his mild businesslike self. "It'll take a while to do the paperwork. If I'm not around when they turn you out, come to the *Belle.*"

"I'll find it," Clint said as the guard shoved him out of the door. He clenched his fists in anger, but didn't raise them. He was getting damned tired of being pushed —both by these guards and deputies, and by people putting him in positions he did not want to be in. He would work for Hutchinson for exactly two months—as long as he could get his work done for Don Carlos at the same time —then the shoe would be on the other foot. He would own the wood yard and Hutchinson would have to deal with him.

As Clint was locked back in his cell Garth Hutchinson made an arrangement with the marshal to release him on Garth's signature, no bail money required. The marshal was a man who would appreciate the fine service the *Belle* would offer when he needed to go to Sacramento or Benicia. He was a man who valued others and their influence, and who knew whose back to scratch to get it.

In less than a half hour, Clint was back on the street, his Navy Colt's back in his holster, his promise to appear at a hearing in two weeks signed and on the marshal's desk. He headed back to the livery, deciding to clean up before he made an appearance at the *Belle*.

He first called on the San Francisco-Benicia-Sacramento Steam Navigation office, and a clerk there informed him that Mr. Hutchinson was aboard the *Belle*. Clint could not help but smile as he mounted the long gangplank and got his feet back on a deck. It had been a long time since he had been a sailor, and boarding the riverboat. even, though she was steam-driven, brought back twelve years of mostly good memories.

Not seeing anyone on the open main deck other than roustabout busily making last touches on her bright work and paint, he climbed a stairway and found the door to the main salon. Entering, he paused and stared about with honest fascination. He had never seen anything to match her. Fitted in only the finest, and clean and neat as a pin. Clint whistled low, then shook his head.

"She really be something, don't she?" The voice came from his right.

"A sight to behold," Clint answered the short stout man, who walked over and stood before him.

"Can I be helpin' you?" he asked.

"I'm looking for Mr. Hutchinson. I'm hired on."

The man extended his hand. "Sean O'Flarraty," he said. Clint shook with him. "Formerly a crew boss on the *Belle*'s refittin', now her purser.

"Clint Ryan. I guess it's your safe I'll be guardin'—I'm, the new master-at-arms." Then he cocked his head and pursed his lips. "Kilkenny, or maybe Tipperary?"

"No, lad. Limerick. But ye not be far off. Then ye know the sainted land?"

"Kilkenny myself, but I've been here in the land of plenty going on twenty years. Except for a time on the sea."

" 'Tis a fine thing, 'tis, to be here, with the famine an' all, but I worry 'bout those at home. Did ye come indentured?"

"I did, as a wee lad, after I lost my ma and pa and a sister on the journey over."

"None of us understand the Lord's ways," Sean said, and rested his hand on Clint's broad shoulder for a moment.

Clint knew that he could probably talk for an hour or a day with this man who came from less than fifty miles from his family home, but he had a payroll to worry about. "So where is Mr. Hutchinson?"

"I think he might be in Miss DuBois's

quarters. In the passageway just behind the stage next to the bar there, lad."

"I thank you, Mr. O'Flarraty," Clint said, and started away.

"Friends call me Stubby . . . and we'll be seeing each other," the squat, balding Irishman called after him.

"Stubby it is, then," Clint said, waving.

He found the door with MISS RACHEL DUBOIS engraved in brass on it, pulled off his hat, and knocked.

He caught his breath when she opened, her hair falling free over her shoulders, emerald eyes centering on him. It was all he could do not to whistle in amazement as he looked over her shoulder into the plush room, all silks and crystal.

"Yes?" she asked, her voice lyrical.

"Sorry to bother you. Looking for Mr. Hutchinson."

"He went on up to the pilothouse."

"Thank you," Clint said, and started to turn.

"And you are?" she questioned.

He turned back. "Ryan. Clint Ryan. I've been hired on as master-at-arms."

She extended her hand and Clint took it. He started to let go, but she hung on, soft and warm, for a moment.

105

"That's a fancy name for guard."

"Yes, ma'am. That's more to the point."

"Then I'll be seeing quite a lot of you, Mr. Ryan." She finally turned his hand loose, but not his eyes, and hers were hypnotic—the most beautiful he had ever seen. "I'm Rachel DuBois, singer and official hostess of the *Belle*."

"Pleased to meet you," Clint said, and meant it. They stood, just looking at each other for a clumsy moment, then Clint backed away. "Thanks for the help." He turned and started away. He felt those emerald eyes on him and didn't hear the door close again until he had rounded the corner and was out of sight.

He found Hutchinson in the pilothouse, talking to an equally well-dressed man. Clint knocked, even though the door was open.

Hutchinson looked up and waved him in. "Ryan, this is Henry Slocumb. Our new master-at-arms, Henry. Mr. Clint Ryan."

Slocumb didn't bother to extend his hand, just nodded and went back to his conversation with Hutchinson.

"I've met Mr. Slocumb," Clint said. "Rather informally, but we've met."

"Really, sir?" Slocumb said. He studied

Clint for a moment, then turned his attention back to Hutchinson. "I doubt it."

"Don't," Clint said, a little irritated at the man's pompous manner. "I dropped a reata over your head while you were bobbin' down the Sacramento."

Slocumb eyed Clint again. It was obvious it was a subject he didn't want to talk about. "Oh," he said, and turned away. "Garth, I think you should consider a stop at—"

Hutchinson interrupted him with a wide smile, turning his attention to Clint. "You pulled our illustrious pilot out of the river like a drowned muskrat?"

"Sure did. He and the *Queen Anne* tangled with the *River Ruler* and he ended up in the drink with fifty or so others. It was a real mess." Clint was merely being honest, but Slocumb was taking it unkindly. His ears were beginning to redden under his wreath of rust-red curls, and his hands balled into fists at his sides.

"That's a coincidence. I'd say you owe him a tall drink, Slocumb," Hutchinson said, smiling broadly and obviously enjoying Slocumb's discomfort.

"Any man would have done the same," Clint offered.

"No, no. Slocumb here owes you, sure as hell's hot."

Clint felt Slocumb's irritation and didn't want to get off to a bad start with the pilot, who was usually lord and master of the boat.

"Show Ryan around," Garth instructed the well-dressed pilot, whose jaw was now tightly clamped. "He's got to know every nook and cranny of the *Belle*." The humor rang obvious in his voice.

Slocumb nodded perfunctorily, brushed by Clint, and strode out the door. Clint said nothing, then turned to follow.

Hutchinson called after him. "I want you to hire on the other two guards today, or by noon tomorrow at the latest." His voice hardened. "Remember, what those men who work for you do is your responsibility, and I'll hold you for their actions . . . so you better hire well."

"Yes, sir," Clint said, but kept on walking. He was uncomfortable with this situation and could not help but think Hutchinson somewhat the fool for purposefully getting two of his key employees off to a bad start.

As he might have expected, he got the fastest tour of the *Belle* ever given while

Slocumb kept the conversation sparse, caustic, and focused on the boat, ignoring Clint's attempts at friendship, and stomping around until the tramp was completed and they had returned to the pilothouse. Clint found Hutchinson gone and excused himself. Slocumb did not bother with a good-bye or a go-to-hell.

Clint finally found his new boss back in his office on Long Wharf. The clerk, an officious little man, kept him waiting outside Hutchinson's private office for a half hour before showing him inside.

Hutchinson didn't look up from his broad cypress desk.

"There's the matter of the Vegas' payroll advance," Clint said, irritation obvious in his voice.

Glancing up from his paperwork with irritation, Hutchinson said, "It's actually not due until Saturday."

"Not correct. The agreement calls for you to advance by Thursday, a week, for the following Saturday, so you're always eight days ahead of the game. Seven hundred fifty dollars every Thursday for six weeks, so long as the work is progressing."

"You've read the agreement," Hutchinson said with a little surprise.

"Sure have."

"Then you know I have to inspect the work and see that it *is* progressing," he lied.

"Not the way I read it. It says you have the *right* to inspect and approve, but still the money's due even if you don't get around to doing an inspection."

Hutchinson began to redden and he worked the muscles in his jaw. "It's been a long time since that agreement was drawn. Tell my clerk, Griswold, to draw a draft and make arrangements to get it delivered to the wood yard—"

"A draft won't do, Mr. Hutchinson. Don Carlos won't have time to go to Sacramento to get a draft cashed and still make the payroll on Saturday."

"Then you take the damned draft to Adams and get it converted to cash, then *you* take the cash to the wood yard . . . after you've hired the guards. Be back sixteen hours after you leave, understand? I'll dock you for the time off."

"Understood." Clint pivoted on his heel and started out.

"And Ryan, make damn sure you get back. I'd hate to think that payroll might go south."

Again Clint spun on his heel and, as

quickly as he'd started out, returned. He strode to the desk, rested his knuckles on it, and leaned over until his face was only two feet from Garth Hutchinson's.

"You and I need to get something straight, Hutchinson. I do what I say I'm gonna do, and I don't like that fact questioned . . . by anyone."

"Then do it," Hutchinson said coldly. "And it's Mr. Hutchinson to you, so long as you're on my payroll. Don't forget, Ryan, you'll be on my payroll until you pay back the five hundred plus interest that I laid out for your bail." He waved a receipt bearing the marshal's letterhead for five hundred dollars in bail money—a piece of stationery Hutchinson had borrowed from the marshal's office and had had his clerk put his fine hand to.

Clint stormed out.

Within the hour Clint had found a man he wanted to hire as one of the guards and signed him on.

Toy Lee Chang was a member of the Tok Loy tong in San Francisco, and Clint had known him for a long time. One of the things about Toy that Clint would not mention to Hutchinson was the fact that he would also gain a certain amount of loyalty from the tong—probably a thousand strong —by employing one of their members, and the Tok Loy tong was preeminent among the many Chinese groups that circulated in the underbelly of the San Francisco waterfront, and more and more, throughout California's goldfields. Not only would Clint gain loyalty, but he would gain an invaluable source of information. Clint believed in having friends in low places, and the Chinese, Mexicans, and Indians were the lifeblood of the menial jobs on the waterfronts and river ways. Clint knew that a great number of the passengers on board the *Belle* would be Chinese, and it would be helpful to have the big man aboard.

Toy was anything but what his name denoted—a barrel of a man, strong as a water buffalo, but still light on his feet and quick. Clint had watched him cut a swath with both a tong hatchet and a Chinese executioner's sword, and had been glad he was not one of the men on the business end of either. For a big man, Toy could do things with his feet that amazed all, particularly those who happened to view the callused bottoms of those large appendages just before they viewed the stars.

112

Although Toy was as silent as he was large and efficient, he was dutiful, would do exactly what he was told—and would never, never be the cause of trouble, only its solution.

By the time Clint returned to the boat with Toy in tow, Griswold had the draft prepared. He gathered it up, then went aboard to introduce Toy to Hutchinson, and to show Toy what he wanted done while he was away at Rancho del Rio Ancho.

He found Hutchinson in Stubby O'Flarraty's purser's office, a cubbyhole on the main deck near the gangplank—but a place that would be the center of Clint's attention on the trips back from Sacramento. It held a six-hundred-pound safe that would carry as much as five hundred pounds of gold at a time. At the going rate of sixteen dollars an ounce for southern goldfield dust, that was eight thousand ounces or $128,000 worth —Clint had carefully calculated it out after his tour. If the shipment held northern California dust, at its lower price of ten dollars an ounce, the shipment would be worth a lot less, but still enough to tempt any of the cloven-hoofed.

Hutchinson asked Clint to wait outside until he finished with Stubby, then after

113

a few minutes stepped out the purser's door.

"Mr. Hutchinson, this is Toy Chang, one of my new guards."

Garth Hutchinson made no move to extend his hand, but did look him up and down before he spoke. "Step inside, Ryan."

Clint followed him into the purser's office. Stubby looked up from his work but, noting the look on Hutchinson 's face, offered Clint no greeting and turned back to the desk.

"Damn, Ryan," Hutchinson began, obviously annoyed, "I had no idea you'd hire some John Chinaman. This boat has a reputation"

"And losing a gold shipment would just about seal that reputation and be about as fatal as a sinking. Toy is as good as they come, won't be recognized as a guard by any white man bent on doing us harm, is loyal as a Saint Bernard and twice as tough . . . and we'll have plenty of his brethren aboard who will jump to his whistle. He's known all over the waterfront and the river." Clint didn't mention his relationship to the tong. Hutchinson didn't have to know everything.

Hutchinson considered this a moment.

"We'll try him for a while if you're set on it. Where's the other man? A decent white man, I trust?"

"White as snow. I'll be bringing him back from Rancho del Rio Ancho."

"Then this Toy will be the only man on board while you're gone?"

"I'll spend some time with Toy before I leave. He doesn't speak much, but don't let that fool you. He understands English perfectly and he'll do exactly what you tell him to."

Clint turned to leave, his hand on the knob, but Hutchinson stopped him. "You didn't have to pay that Chinee any fifteen dollars a week. I don't suppose you're considering cutting out a piece of that thirty I allotted for yourself?"

Clint turned back and spoke evenly. "He'll earn what he's paid, and when I decide to take more than my share, you'll be the first to know." He closed the door behind him just a little harder than necessary.

Within the hour Clint had shown Toy the boat and let him know what was expected of him—which was mainly keeping sightseers and gawkers off the *Belle* until they began operation—and was on his way from Adam's Express, where he had cashed Hutchinson's draft and placed Don Carlos's money in a canvas money belt. With seven hundred fifty dollars in gold coin in a canvas belt around his waist, he headed back to the wharves. The *River Ruler* was making its alternate-day run to Sacramento, and Clint could just make it. Traveling aboard her would give him not only transportation to the wood yard, but a chance to watch and talk with her master-at-arms, and to get a better feeling for his own new, hopefully short-term, job.

He did learn some things on the trip up the river, some of them good, some of them bad—the worst being that the *Ruler* would not even pause as they passed Honker Bay and the wood yard. Clint waited until they neared the shore beyond the bay's inlet, rolled his boots into his shirt, and dived off the boat to swim ashore. The weight of the seven hundred fifty dollars in gold coin in the money belt, combined with the shirt and boots he carried, had him heaving deeply as he sat back on the mud bank to pull his wet boots back on.

It was the better part of a mile back to the wood yard. The sun was setting, casting a golden haze over the bay and steaming tules, ducks and geese made their last circles of the evening before sitting down in the bay's center, and the men were just breaking for the day when he arrived. He asked one of the *carreta* drivers to wait up so he could ride to the hacienda with him, then sought out Boulders Blanchard.

Blanchard was sitting around a fire with his rivermen, camped away from the rest of the crew, sipping a steaming tin of black coffee when Clint sauntered up and sat beside him.

Boulders eyed him over his coffee cup.

"You a-lookin' for another lesson in the art of the knuckle and knee?" Blanchard said with a wide grin.

"If that's the only way I can get you to come back to San Francisco with me, it'll have to do."

"Then there's a good chance your a-gonna get whipped like a stepchild. Why the hell would I want to go back to that scumhole?"

"Twenty dollars a week, living the life of a potentate on board the fanciest boat on the river, that's why. You do know something about river work, don't you, Blanchard?"

Boulders smiled even wider than he had

at the thought of a fistfight. "Get this man a cup of that hull varnish. Tell me more, son."

In fifteen minutes, Clint was on his way to the hacienda. Hutchinson had been right about Clint not having to pay Toy the fifteen a week allotted to him, but Clint knew he would have to pay Boulders more than that, so it evened out, and the ten he had paid the big Chinese was twice what he had been making as a stevedore. Clint didn't mind that Boulders would be making as much as he was, so long as Boulders knew who was the boss. Clint didn't feel exactly right about Toy making less, as the two men would be doing the same job, but maybe he could find a way to make it right before he left the boat.

Don Carlos Vega was not happy when Clint arrived at the hacienda.

"I had hoped you would be in Monterey by now," he said, his old brows furrowing even more than they did naturally.

"You gave me two jobs, Don Carlos. I'll go after the second one tomorrow."

"Then eat and rest, and be on your way early."

"Before the sun," Clint said, but the old man was still not reassured.

Later that night, after the usual ten o'clock supper, they had all retired, and when Clint was almost asleep, a gentle tapping at the door jolted him upright. He pulled on his *calzonevas* and made his way quietly to the door, tripped the latch, and swung it aside.

Apolonia Vega, barefoot, clad only in a robe over something silk—showing plenty of cleavage—slipped into the room and pushed the door shut behind her.

"Is anything wrong?" Clint whispered, suddenly conscious that he wore no shirt.

"Nothing," she whispered a little breathlessly. "Only I haven't gotten a chance to speak to you alone since you returned from the Kaweah. The old men take all of your time." She rested a hand on his bare chest as she spoke, and her warmth flooded through him. Even in the darkness, he could make out the pout on her lips, and it wasn't unattractive.

"Your father?"

"They are all asleep."

"You put me in a bad spot, Apolonia. This is Don Carlos's home, and I am a guest . . . a trusted guest." Clint's allegiance was being strained as much as the fabric of his trousers.

"This is my house, too. Would you feel so much the guest if we were to . . . to talk, in the *establo*. My mare would be my duenna and see that there was no impropriety." He could see her eyes light with mischief, the pout teasingly increase, and could feel his resolve flow away like the Sacramento.

"I guess that would be all right, so long as you have a chaperon to watch over you. She is a very prudish mare, isn't she?"

Apolonia ignored his attempt at humor. "Then meet me in the barn." She spun on her heel, not awaiting an answer, and slipped out of the room.

Clint pulled his shirt and boots on and, rather than follow out the door and down through the patio, waited a few moments then slipped out the shuttered but unglazed window.

Apolonia was waiting, a small taper lit and burning in a rusty sconce on a post next to the hay pile, where she sat without ceremony on two saddle blankets she had spread out, her legs crossed in a less than ladylike, almost tomboyish, manner. He walked quietly across the wide barn and took a seat next to her, watching a door that opened into a lean-to—a door to the room where his friend Sancho Guiterrez slept—Sancho Guiterrez, with whom, along with Don Carlos Vega, he had just had dinner, sitting across from the girl who reclined on the hay next to him. He had the sudden urge to scramble to his feet and hurry back to his room . . . but she smelled of lilac, and must have read his thoughts, because her full lower lip quivered.

"Are you sorry you came?" she asked.

"A silly question," he said in a low tone, but it had been a very good question.

"I have thought of you often since you rescued me from that cruel sea captain. He was a dreadful man."

"You owe me nothing, Apolonia. Your father—"

"I know. My father paid you in horses." She reached up and touched his cheek with a warm hand, and looked directly into his eyes. "And I did not invite you here because I owed you. I am here because here is where I wish to be, and I hope you are also."

Her face came nearer, and there was nothing to do but kiss her . . . so he did.

It was gray-skied, just before the sun rose, by the time he got back to his room.

Clint packed his bedroll quickly, found

his way to the *cocina,* where two old women were already slapping tortillas, packed a half-dozen filled with beef and peppers into a muslin sack, and went to the barn to borrow a fast horse. For some reason he wanted to be out of there long before Don Carlos arose.

Sancho was already forking hay to the family's horses that resided in the barn. He turned and eyed Clint, not speaking, as he entered.

"Buenos dias, amigo," Clint offered.

"I've seen better days," Sancho replied without turning away from his job.

"I need a horse."

"My reata is on the post there." Sancho motioned with a shrug of his shoulder. "You carry the name Lazo and should know its use. There are horses in the corral outside. You know where the tack is."

He still hadn't turned. Clint gathered up the reata and walked out to the corral that held the remuda for the working vaqueros, picked out a tall dappled gray, and dropped a loop over its head, then returned to the *establo.*

He curried the gray, who kicked up his heels and shied at first, then settled down.

"This one has plenty of fire," Clint commented to Sancho, who continued his work without speaking.

After a moment, he set the fork aside and turned, folding his arms across his chest. "He is a strong Spanish horse. All things Spanish are full of fire, but that fire can be quenched and they can be beaten down, hurt so the fire never rises again. Handle my horse with care, Lazo . . . as I pray you will all things from Rio Ancho."

Clint studied the man's hard eyes for a long moment, then answered in a soft voice. "I have the greatest respect for all things from Rio Ancho, Sancho. I would do nothing to hurt them. Any of them."

"That is a good thing, Lazo. *Vaya con Dios.*" Sancho turned and walked out of the barn.

"Take care," Clint said. He mounted, gave his heels to the tall gray, and headed for the wood yard. He knew the window to Apolonia's room and studied it as he passed. He felt more than saw that she was watching him through the shutters. Clint tipped his broad-brimmed hat at the window just in case, and the shutter opened and a fine-fingered hand waved.

They had already said their good-byes.

By nightfall, having ridden double down

the shore to pick up the *River Ruler* at Benicia for her return trip, he, Boulders Blanchard, and the dappled gray were aboard the *Belle*. Clint spent a couple of hours acquainting Boulders with the boat and, more important, convincing him to listen and not talk, and certainly not crow, while doing his job as a boat guard. The object, Clint informed him, was to keep the passengers alive and well and paying for booze or gambling—not beaten to a pulp. He also requested that Boulders not throw the gawkers and trespassers off into the bay, but rather escort them politely down the gangplank—at least the first time.

He also assured him that there was no need to prove he could whip Toy Chang —though he knew that Boulders could prattle on for hours and not intimidate or even irritate the big Chinese—for they were shipmates. The two would surely kill each other, or at least maim each other for life, if they ever came to blows.

Even after the two hours of careful instruction, Clint still fell asleep with a certain trepidation about leaving the two men in charge.

Now he had to get some sleep, then ride or find a coastal schooner for Monterey.

And hope that no one there remembered that John Clinton Ryan was a man wanted for negligence in the wreck of an American brig and the loss of fourteen men.

And he wondered if, upon his return to Rancho del Rio Ancho, Don Carlos would welcome him as he had so many times before, and keep his bargain for the wood yard.

The way Clint felt at the moment, a grab bag of emotions, he almost wished he would not.

6

Before dawn Clint was prowling the water-front, looking for a schooner. The trip down the California coast a sailing ship could be five times as fast as the trip back up, due to the prevailing winds, so he wanted a ship he could take both Diablo and the dappled gray aboard so he could come back overland. The only coastal schooner sailing was a sixty-five-footer that had no provisions for stock. He hoped the gray to the livery, paid his bill, saddled Diablo, and put a lead rope on the gray, then they were off down the peninsula on the grueling ride to Monterey. He hoped Diablo wasn't barn sour from so much time in the stall, but the big horse proved his worth and set the pace for the gray.

Keeping the thickly timbered Santa Cruz Mountains to his right, and the San Francisco Bay with its thousands of gulls, then its brackish marsh and birds of a thousand varieties to his left, and skirting San Jose, he made the north end of the Santa Clara Valley by noon. He rode at a steady lope, and every hour changed horses and rested only as long as it took to leisurely resaddle the well-lathered horses or occasionally water them where opportunity and a fresh trickle allowed. Finding a grassy slope leading down to Arroyo del Coyote, he stopped, rested, resaddled, and visited with a shepherd who tended a flock of sheep from Rancho San Antonio.

He passed few travelers, and only touched his hat brim as he did so, not breaking stride, though it seemed most of them wanted news of the trail ahead. He forged on at a steady lope.

Just before nightfall, every muscle in his body crying for relief, he noticed a hovel with a smoking stone stack in a grove of mountain mahogany and turned off Camino Real. Calling out, "Hola la casa! Hello the house!" he reined up in front.

An old vaquero greeted him; seeing the condition of the tired horses, he insisted Clint stay and spend the night. Clint discovered it was an outrider's shack for Rancho, Salsipuedes, one of the major ranchos in the newly formed county of Santa Cruz. The vaquero informed him he was over two-thirds of the way to Monterey, having ridden over ninety miles that day. The long summer day, good grass and water, and the flat country had made it seem like less. Still he was exhausted. The old man tended the horses, and Clint fell asleep while the vaquero prepared a simple meal of beans and tortillas.

The morning came early. The odor of coffee awakened him. The *viejo* had the palomino saddled and the lead rope on the gray by the time Clint filled his coffee tin, had his boots on, and got outside. For the old man's trouble, he offered him a coin, then was afraid he had offended the proud vaquero. He should have known better. Leaving a new friend, he crossed Rio de Pajaro by the time the sun burned the morning gold to clear blue, then waded Rio Salinas in the wide marshgrass and tule-covered flats of the north end of the Salinas Valley.

At a little before noon, knowing it was that time by both the position of the sun and the vacant flapping of his stomach against his backbone, he sat on a rise overlooking Monterey and the long, low, flagged-cypress-covered point beyond. The bay had over a dozen ships anchored in it, with a lumber boat pulling alongside the new wharf to unload its redwood and spruce from the Russian River cuttings, and the Pacific mail steamer huffing and puffing away as Clint studied the village becoming a city.

It was Saturday, a workday, and he knew that the members of the Land Commission would be in their meeting. He should have plenty of time to find livery for the horses and a roof for himself prior to the end of the session.

He found an adobe with a small sign, JUANITA'S COCINA and tied the horses to the rail in front, loosening the cinch on the gray, which had carried him the last few miles into the village. The horses had eaten along the way, while he had been limited to the old man's small portion of frijoles and tortillas.

As soon as he pulled away the cowhide that covered the doorway, he paused, closed his eyes, and inhaled deeply in appreciation. He knew he had come to the right place. Just outside the backdoor of the small café, he saw a cooking pit with a metal grill. A variety of pots were located on the grill and the odors that emanated from them, some in roiling steam, promised what was to come.

He sat at one of the many plank tables and smiled at the approaching woman. She had obviously partaken of the succulent dishes often, since she waddled over, melon-sized breasts straining to escape from her red-dyed *jerga* blouse.

"Buenos dias," she said, grinning at her early customer.

"Feed me, *señora, por favor,"* Clint said simply, and the woman beamed and hurried away.

She returned with a trayful of steaming delights, setting them in front of him. He recognized the tortillas and frijoles and salsa, but when he looked quizzically at the other bowls, she explained each dish with a point of a stout finger whose joints bulged.

Cordero cabazo, lamb's head; *migas,* sour bread sliced thin and fried in garlic oil until crisp; *pastel de tamal,* a pie of onion, garlic, chicken meat, beef roast, corn, tomatoes, peppers, and olives, richly spiced, and served in a masa cheese crust; *mostaza,* wild mustard greens in olive oil and garlic; *pie cerdo,* pig's foot.

Clint smiled and said, *"con vino, pot-favor,"* and the woman hurried away for a mug of wine. After eating enough to last him for two days, he pushed away from the table as a group of well-dressed men entered.

Clint picked his hat off the table and fitted it on his head pulling it low over his eyes.

One of the men spoke, and it was as if he had struck Clint on the head with the table leg. First shock then cold trembling anger racked Clint's backbone. He hoisted the Navy Colt's in its holster to make sure it rode free and easy and, without thinking, checked to see that his ten-inch knife was sheathed at his left side.

He had been worried about the warrant for his arrest being brought to light. Now he was as sure it would be as if it were centered in the beam of the new lighthouse being constructed on Punta Piños, where Monterey Bay began.

The tallest man among the five had reason to know of the warrant more than any other in California—he was the liar who had caused it to be issued, Captain Quade Sharpentier. Older, slightly grayer, with more lines around the eyes, but just as gruff and rawhide lean, Sharpentier took a seat with four other men. He no longer looked the sea captain, but now more resembled a politician with his gold-handled walking stick, fine blue coat, waistcoat of regal purple silk and gold buttons, white shirt and black cravat, and gray trousers over well-shined boots. He carried a high hat, and carefully set it on a nearby windowsill.

Clint felt his eyes center on him, but the anticipated shout of recognition, and call to arms, did not come.

The captain appeared to be unarmed, should it come to that, but Clint knew he would be carrying a belly gun either in an inside coat pocket or pushed into his belt, and the walking stick probably hid a blade.

As much as Clint wanted to stand and confront the man, he decided he had best bide his time. He had a job to do, and he damn well couldn't do it from a jail cell. Even after he settled the debt he owed Sharpentier, there were still four men left, and he had no intention of harming some innocent bystander—and the odds were substantially against him, should they elect to involve themselves. He allowed the tremor of anger to settle, dug into his trousers pocket, and dropped a tiny dollar gold piece on the table—probably twice what the bill was—and made his way to the door.

"You have change," the woman called from behind him, but he ignored her and went on to the horses, cinched up the gray, and mounted. He spun the gray away, but stopped when he heard his name ring out.

"Ryan!"

He reined the horse back to face the cowhide-covered doorway of Juanita's Cocina, his hand resting on the butt of his Navy Colt's. Quade Sharpentier stepped out.

"Captain," Clint snarled through clinched teeth.

"I'm a captain no longer. I'm staying at the Four Winds near the old customs house. Come, by there about nine o'clock tonight. I want to talk to you.

"I'd as soon shoot you down like the dog you are, right here."

Sharpentier flashed a coyote grin. "There's law here now, Ryan. You'll hang for shooting down an unarmed and respected citizen of Monterey. We've got things to get settled, so you'll be there at nine if you know what's good for you."

Now he had Clint's curiosity aroused. "I wouldn't miss the opportunity. You're planning to be armed, I hope?"

133

"Not a chance, and I'll have a witness or two there, so you plan on keeping that iron where it belongs holstered. Nine o'clock." He turned and the cowhide flapped closed behind him.

"You son of a bitch," Clint muttered as he reined away.

But he would be there at nine.

He found a livery and got the horses taken care of, made arrangements to sleep in the tack room, then went hunting the Land Commission meeting. By the time he had located Government House—with a dozen buckboards and buggies, twice that many horses and a couple of fine calèches tied outside—he was surprised to see Quade Sharpentier among the delegates going into the afternoon session.

Well, Sharpentier has come a long way since the days of the brig Savannah, *Clint thought. Lying, cheating, and stealing all the way, I would bet.*

He wanted to find a cantina and sip *aguardiente* until the meeting was over, but decided he couldn't do his job if he did. He wanted to talk straight and get the hell out of Monterey and back to San Francisco, back to the Kaweah as quickly as he could. Instead, he walked out into the center of the square and settled down under a wide live oak. Leaning on its rough trunk in the dark shade, he pulled his hat low over his eyes, took a deep cleansing breath of Monterey's ocean breeze, and acted like a true Californio—he took a siesta.

Clint stood waiting as the meeting broke up.

He knew a number of the men who exited the large adobe Government House, but sought out one advocate, Edward Beale, whom he knew would have more influence than most. Ned Beale had been one of the heroes of the Battle of San Pasqual, and Clint had fought side by side with the navy officer. Clint had heard that Beale was on leave from the navy, had associated himself with a New York financier William Aspinwall, and was in the cattle business with John Frémont and the freight business with Aspinwall.

He cornered Beale, who greeted him warmly. They chatted for a moment, then Clint got to the point. "I'm here at the request of Don Carlos Vega."

"I know of Rancho del Rio Ancho," Beale said quickly.

"He's concerned about the title to the family property."

"One of those who didn't refile after the fire?" Beale asked.

"Yes. What can I do to assure him there will be no problem?"

"You can't." Beale shook his head in concern.

"That rancho has been in his family for several generations."

"Every one of the old dons' titles are being investigated. I would suggest you gather a voluminous file of depositions regarding his family's continuous occupancy of the property, return it here, and make sure it comes to the attention of the commission."

"Is there time?"

"I'll see that his title is not on the agenda of the committee for two weeks. That should give you more than enough time."

Clint extended his hand. "Thank you, Ned."

"This kind of thing is what we're here for, Clint. You tell Don Carlos that I helped. I'll call on him soon, as I plan to run for Congress—from the southern portion of California, but I'll need all the help I can get."

"I'll be back with all the written testimony I can gather."

"The more the better, Clint, and the sooner the better," Beale said, his manner serious. "There are men here who seek any excuse to dispossess the Mexicans. I suggest you collect all the Anglo testimony you can. Call on Larkin for sure; you met Larkin. His word will weigh heavily in the old don's favor."

Great. Clint thought sarcastically. Thomas Larkin had been the American consul, when California was a Mexican possession, who had issued warrant for Clint's arrest. He would be seriously pressing his luck to call on the man. But if it had to be done . . .

Beale had a dinner party to attend and excused himself. Clint continued to circulate among the members, making sure he renewed as many old acquaintances as possible, then wandered out to the town square. Some of the members retired to a nearby hotel bar, and Clint did the same, but didn't drink. He would need all of his faculties for his coming meeting with Sharpentier.

As the other men continued to drink, Clint ate a bowl of stew and a chunk of thick-crusted bread and listened to the talk, then, bored with it, made his way out to walk along the beach. The night was warm, fogless, and the night sounds—the breaking surf and murmur of wind in the cypress— soothing. It was a good place to think.

Why did the captain want to talk with him? Sharpentier had laid the blame on him for the sinking of the *Savannah,* and done a damn good job of it. He had been the one who got Larkin to issue the warrant, lying to the consul in order to cover his own malfeasance. Maybe he wanted to put the matter to rest. If so, Clint was more than willing. It was a thorn in his side, and if he wanted to become a landowner in California, he had no choice. It would mean he would not get his revenge on the man who had caused him so much trouble, but then again, who knew? Maybe sometime in the future . . . The Good Lord had a way of making things equal out. A man who did a lot of bad usually got more than his share of headache and heartache in return.

Finally Clint decided it was time and headed for the Four Winds. The hotel was one of the newer structures in Monterey, located near the old customs house and very near the beach. Two stories tall, of redwood with a number of expensive glazed windows, it was one of the two fine new hotels in the burgeoning town.

Clint paused on the porch, made sure his Navy Colt's was loaded and dry, and entered. A few of the commission members stood in the parlor, sipping brandy, smoking, and talking. Clint walked to the desk and informed the clerk he was there to see Quade Sharpentier, then walked to a unoccupied corner of the parlor and waited. It was only a moment until the captain entered and walked directly to Clint, extending his hand.

"I'll pass on the handshake, Sharpentier. What's on your mind?"

Anger flickered across the captain's gray eyes like a vulture's shadow, but the man recovered quickly. "Brandy, or a whiskey?" he asked, a smile cutting a thin line in his hard face.

"I'll pass. What's on your mind?"

Sharpentier took a seat in one of two wingback chairs in the corner of the room and waved Clint into the other. Clint almost refused, but he wanted this matter resolved. Reluctantly, he sat.

"Now, Ryan, it's time we buried the hatchet—"

"Not a bad idea, Captain. How 'bout I bury it between your lying shoulders?"

"Very humorous. I'm serious—"

"You think I'm not?"

"Ryan, my report was filed based on the testimony of the crew."

"Lie! Your report was filed based on your trying to save your own skin with the owners. You know damned well that I had come off a twenty-four-hour watch and was in my bunk when we took that reef. You boys had been keepin' warm at the grog keg and it was your fault—the officers' fault—that we were off course."

"That's all behind us now."

"Easy for you to say. As far as I know, a warrant is still outstanding for my arrest."

Sharpentier's eyes narrowed as he dug a cigar out of his waistcoat pocket. "Smoke?" he offered.

"No."

The captain lit up, eyeing Clint as he did so. He exhaled a plume of smoke. "That's true, the warrant is still in effect, and I guess you would like to see that warrant recalled."

"Of course."

"I've heard about you several times over

the past five years, Ryan. I hear you have a certain amount of influence with the old Mexican families?"

"I've earned their trust," Clint said, being more frank than usual.

"I can use a man who can influence the dons."

"What you're saying is that if I help you, you'll do what you damn well know is right and should have already done—get the warrant recalled." Clint arose slowly as he spoke until he stood tall over the reclining figure. His voice swelled with every word. "You are truly a son of a bitch," he almost shouted. The rest of the room quieted and the men stared in their direction.

"Sit down, Ryan," Sharpentier advised quietly, clamping the cigar tightly in his teeth.

Clint glanced at the other men, then let his balled fists relax and sank back to the chair. The others took up their conversations again.

"Don't be a fool, Ryan," the captain began again. "You've got something I want, and I've got something you want. It's only good business to do a little trading."

Lie down with dogs and you get fleas, Clint

thought, but didn't say it. He wanted that damned warrant recalled.

He sighed deeply. "What's on your mind?"

"Land. Land is on my mind. I want you to act as my agent to buy up some of the old ranchos. Frémont just bought several thousand acres for sixteen thousand dollars. I want those kinds of buys. And you're one of the few gringos these Mexes trust."

"I know Rancho Mariposa. Frémont stole it."

"Exactly. You get me even one buy like that, and I'll see that the warrant is recalled, and pay you, say, two percent as a finder's fee."

"That's one way to solve our mutual problem," Clint said, his tone hardening. "The other way would be to pull this Colt's and shoot your lying ass off."

Sharpentier managed a smug smile. "That wouldn't get the warrant removed."

Clint sat in silence for a moment. "You find a neutral party, an attorney or judge, file a statement retracting your former charges and requesting that the warrant be recalled. I'll help you find a rancho that fills the bill . . . but I won't use any of your tactics to do so, Sharpentier. A willing seller at a good price, that's all I'll promise. And it'll cost you eight percent."

"Five."

"Deal."

"Then that's good enough," the captain said with a look of triumph in his eyes. Of course, the statement won't be made available to you until such time as you're successful in finding me such a property."

"You dictate and have the recision witnessed, let me read it, and we'll agree on a mutual party to hold it. When you acquire a rancho, the document will be turned over to me."

"Good enough." Again Sharpentier extended his hand. As if reaching for a viper, Clint took it, shook once, and dropped it as he would have a leper's.

"Now," Sharpentier continued, "let's talk about land. I represent a group of men from the East. We call ourselves the Golden West Land and Cattle Company—"

Clint sat and listened to what the captain was after for better than an hour, and surmised all that what the man wanted was probably impossible to obtain. But so long as he was thought to be helping the captain, the captain would be silent regarding the

143

warrant, and Clint could move forward to get his work done.

With a very sour taste in his mouth, and feeling absolutely dejected, Clint left the Four Winds and made his way back to the livery. Again, he was doing something he didn't want to do for a man he didn't want to be involved with. That was the bad side. Even worse, it was all he could do not to shoot the man down like a cur. The good side was it was another opportunity to make a substantial amount of money.

Still, it didn't set well. Somehow the money already smelled tainted, and he didn't even have it yet, if he ever would.

With the dawn, he was on the trail again, riding Diablo at a lope and trailing the dappled gray.

Late the next afternoon Clint made one stop in the city of San Francisco before he returned to the *Belle*. Clifford Stanhope was a well-known attorney in the city and Clint had two matters to take up with him.

After keeping him cooling his heels for an hour, Stanhope's clerk appeared in his waiting area. "Mr. Ryan, Mr. Stanhope has requested that you come back tomorrow," the youngish fair-haired man reported with officious politeness.

"Can't do that. I've got work to do my-self."

The man disappeared for a moment, then returned. "Mr. Stanhope asked if you can join him for supper. He's got a meeting in an hour, but—"

"Supper would be fine."

Still, it was fifteen minutes before the man appeared. The Seth Thomas pendulum clock on the entry wall showed 6:15. Portly, with great gray muttonchop sideburns framing a round face and bushy gray brows that made his blue eyes appear deep in his face, Stanhope brushed through the entry and waved at Clint. Clint leaped to his feet, and had to stride out to keep up with the shorter man, who checked his pocket watch.

"What's your problem, Mr. Ryan?" he asked as they made their way down the office stairs to the street. Stanhope eyed Clint up and down, as if he wondered if Clint could pay his fee even if he had a problem Stanhope could help with. Covered with trail dust, his *jerga* shirt and *calzonevas* lined with sweat, the man was in dire need of a little soap and water.

"I've been on the trail for two hard days,"

Clint, reading his expression, offered a little self-consciously.

"I don't judge a man by his feathers," Stanhope said, and strode on, again pulling his gold pocket watch from his waistcoat pocket and checking the time.

Even as late as it was, Montgomery Street bustled with freight wagons and horse-backers. A Mexican boy herded a half-dozen goats down the middle of the street, and Chinese men in black robes, with their queues hanging down to the middle of their backs, shuffled along. Men in multicolored shirts with brown canvas pants stuffed into brogans, packs on their backs and pistols and belt hatchets at their waist, carried shovels and picks that identified their hoped-for vocations as new gold-miner millioniares. San Francisco never stopped, even at night.

"Two things, Mr. Stanhope. One problem is mine, one is Don Carlos Vega's."

Stanhope walked only a half block, then turned into a clapboard building with a sign proclaiming FRANÇOIS CHOP AND OYSTER EMPORIUM. Clint felt his mouth water at the thought of a thick pork chop and a plate full of potatoes, but Stanhope walked to a bar where a man shucked oysters and passed them to a line of other men in city coats.

"Give us a dozen each and two mugs of Mad Dog!" Stanhope yelled to the bartender, whose eyes lighted in acknowledgment.

"Yes, sir, Mr. Stanhope."

Clint followed the man to a small round table and sat across from him while he checked his watch for the third time. "We've only got a few minutes, Mr. Ryan," he said.

Clint launched into his story. "Five years ago, then consul Thomas Larkin issued a warrant for my arrest at the request of Captain Sharpentier of the brig *Savannah*."

"A warrant never served?" Stanhope raised his eyebrows.

"A warrant I've managed to avoid, but a false charge." Stanhope eyed him as if he had heard that allegation far too often. "A false charge," Clint repeated with ardor.

"And you want me to defend you against this allegation?"

"No, sir," Clint said, and Stanhope looked surprised. "Sharpentier has agreed to rescind his false allegations if I perform some services for him."

"I'm not sure that's legal," Stanhope said, staring down at the table, thinking.

147

"To rescind charges?" Clint asked incredulously.

"No . . . to charge for rescinding charges."

"I don't give a damn about that. I just want the warrant recalled." Clint went on to explain that he wanted Stanhope to oversee the process and make sure the document Sharpentier drew up would do the job, then he continued with the Vegas' problem while they finished off the raw oysters and the mugs of ale.

"You'll need help with the affidavits," Stanhope said, wiping his mouth with a linen napkin. "The young man who you saw in my anteroom is one of my clerks. He'll accompany you and take the sworn statements regarding the Vegas' claim to Rancho del Rio Ancho, and make sure they're in legal form, properly executed, and witnessed. I see no problem protecting Vega's rights . . . but then again, this damned Land Commission is made up of human beings, and they are fallible."

Stanhope checked his watch then rose, even though Clint had not finished his oysters and beer. "I'll require a two-hundred-dollar retainer. I charge ten dollars per hour for Robert Miles's time—he's my clerk—and my time is charged out at twenty."

Clint couldn't keep the shock from showing on his face.

"That's the rate," Stanhope defended. "Have the retainer at my office tomorrow if you want us to help . . . and the fee will probably be more by the time it's over." Stanhope tipped his hat and left Clint staring at his unfinished oysters, without the appetite to finish them even though he had been starving when he came in. He wiped his mouth and started to rise when an aproned waiter hurried over, his hand extended in anticipation.

"That's three dollars, sir."

Clint stared at him for a moment, then at the disappearing Stanhope, then fished the last five-dollar gold piece he had out of his pocket and handed it over. The only other money he had left was buried behind the rough shack he and Gideon had begun on the Kaweah Ranch, a good hard five-day ride away. Stanhope was right; people were fallible. If they weren't, attorneys would be about as desirable and useful as a wart on a pretty woman's nose.

This retainer was another problem he would have to solve, but hell, he was getting used to it.

He made his way to the *Belle,* fog creeping

149

into the city's dark streets. Two blocks from the waterfront, three burly Sidney Ducks, Turkish mustaches marking them, stepped out of a pitch-black alley in front of him, possibly bent on doing him harm. Clint snatched his Colt's out of its holster without hesitation and ratcheted the hammer back, centering the big barrel on the closest man.

"I'd just as soon blow you all to hell as give you my last two dollars," Clint roared. Wide-eyed, the three men faded quickly back into the alley and Clint stormed on by.

Trying to take two lousy dollars from a crazy man didn't seem to be to their liking.

7

Fog blanketed the bay and an eerie glowing ring circled the anchor light as Clint made his way up the *Belle*'s gangplank. He waved to Toy, who was standing night watch, then found his way to the crew's quarters and to the small nook that was the only semblance of privacy for his and another man's bunks. Each pair of stacked bunks was separated from pairs on either side by eighteen-inch stub walls, where a man could hang his gear, mount a mirror, or strop a razor. The crew's quarters, ten cubbyholes, were located just behind Stubby's small purser's office, and were the only enclosed area on the main deck. The only other enclosed area on the ship was the aft engine room.

Clint collapsed without bothering to undress, too tired to sleep. Instead, he thought about the boat, and how to protect her. Provisions had been made for a crew of twenty who had actual bunks on board the boat—the engineers, the deck chief, the master-at-arms, and the guards, the bartenders and the on-staff gamblers. The rest of the deck crew slept where they might. The boat was configured with her first deck being the main. Her second was confusingly called the main cabin, or salon deck in the area where it was enclosed. Forward of the enclosed area, on the same level, was the hurricane deck, and aft, the boiler deck—even though the boilers were located forward on the main deck below and the engine was aft on the main deck, under the boiler deck. It was all very confusing to a landlubber, which Clint was a long ways from being. Above the salon and king over all was the pilothouse. Completely enclosed on four sides with glass, the pilot had a three-hundred-and-sixty-degree view. The only parts of the boat that dared rise above him were the twin stacks, two forty-foot-long square-timber grasshopper staffs that were used to hop or jack the boat off mud banks, two forward derricks used to load freight, and an aft steam escape pipe. The side wheels were driven by two massive walking beams, and each wheel was eighteen feet in diameter with thirteen six-foot paddles. The boat was forty feet wide, plus the side wheel, which added width—the only disadvantage compared with a stern wheeler.

Passengers on the main deck, the lowest deck containing the lowest form of life—men and animals—slept and ate where they might among the freight and cords of wood that drove the boat. On the salon deck things were entirely different. This deck held twelve private passenger cabins, each named for a state and consequently called staterooms, separate sitting rooms and parlors for men and women—although, since Rachel would most often be the only woman aboard, the women's quarters would be used by men passengers. There were also a large gambling hall and saloon, and a kitchen with a gang table to feed the crew away from the main salon, where meals of eight main dishes—including beef, pork, lamb, fish, wild game—and a dozen side dishes would be prepared for the salon passengers as part of their twelve-dollar fare; the deck passengers were provided soup and bread for an extra charge.

Privies were located aft, where waste fell directly into the water from both the boiler deck—aft of the salon—and the main. Cabins boasted private privies, and Garth Hutchinson was very proud of their design. An eight-inch water trough ran the length of the outside deck, and by merely opening a small cover in each cabin, a passenger discovered a polished wooden toilet seat. Under each, a stream of water continually flowed, pumped by the engines. It was the absolute latest in passenger comfort.

Unloaded, the *Belle* could pass safely though four feet of water. Loaded with two hundred tons of freight, forty passengers in private facilities, and as many men, horses, mules, donkeys, sheep, pigs, and goats as could be crowded aboard her decks, she could pass through seven feet.

Explosion was her greatest fear, and a steam line, often subject to a break, ran from her two boilers forward to her two engines aft. That loud sound was most feared, and the noise from her steam whistle the most loved—except for one other. Garth Hutchinson had a surprise for the river. A steam calliope had been under wraps on the aft boiler deck, and a man had been brought all the way from St. Louis to play it.

Not only would the two notes of her whistle announce her coming, but the calliope would whistle her praises to all who would listen.

As Clint tried to sleep he could not help but feel a touch of admiration for Garth Hutchinson. The man had accomplished a great deal. He was a hard man, with hard ways, but maybe that was what it took. Clint vowed to try to think better of the man. After all, he was taking his money, and he owed him his allegiance.

Finally, hoping that things would start going his way, he fell into a deep sleep.

"God damn the bloody flies!" The voice seemed to surround him. Clint sat up quickly, rapping his head soundly on the top of the bunk. He dropped back, closed his eyes, and rubbed the growing lump.

"You bloody bastards get up off your dead asses and get to work!" The voice rasped at him like a file across his teeth. Clint rolled out of the bunk and stood.

Garth Hutchinson stood berating the men in the crew's cabin.

"What time is it?" Clint managed.

"So the prodigal son has returned," Hutchinson snapped, walking over to where Clint stood rubbing the knot on his head.

"Got in last night," Clint mumbled.

"A day late and a dollar short, I imagine."

"What's eating you?" Clint asked, as Hutchinson had been far too close to the truth. Actually, he was far more than a dollar short of what he needed to solve both his own and the Vegas' problems.

"I'm bloody well ruined, that's what's eating me," Hutchinson snarled, then turned and stomped off. He paused and turned back. "Get up to the office and give me a report on the wood yard—not that it matters much."

Boulders Blanchard stepped out of his own cubbyhole and yawned widely, then walked over to Clint and extended his hand. Clint shook.

"What's his problem?" Clint asked.

"Last night the ol' California Steam Navigation Company announced that rates to Sacramento would be fifty cents a head beginning Friday hence, an' freight fifty cents a hundredweight. There's posters all over the city. Hutchinson had Toy and me a-goin' all over and rippin' 'em down until the boys with the badges jumped us."

"Fifty cents? That's some drop from three dollars."

"So happens, Friday is the maiden voyage of the *Belle*," Boulders said, a wide grin on his face. "Seems like the ol' CSNC is bound and determined to break our Mr. New York Hutchinson. Garth has renamed them Chicken Shit Navigation Company, but he don't smile when he says it."

"You don't seem too brokenhearted," Clint said.

"I'll tell you." Boulders rubbed his stubbled chin. "That man has come about a gnat's ass away from getting his own whipped several times while you was gone. I only been hangin' on here 'cause I tol' you I would . . . an' I promised not to deep-six anyone while you was away. Otherwise, Mr. Hutchinson woulda been the first man in the drink."

Clint stifled a laugh. "The man does seem to attract animosity like flies to a road apple."

"I don't know nothin' about ami—animo—hell, I don't know nothin' about that, but he sure about attracted a brogan up his butt mor'n once since you been gone."

"Well, Boulders, don't forget the twenty a week. I'm gonna go talk with Hutchinson as soon as I get some of this trail dust out of my ears. I'll keep him off you. How's Toy getting on?"

"He's quite a boy, that Toy. He jus' does his job and keeps his mouth shut. I never saw the like."

Again Clint had to laugh. "No, I guess you didn't. Speaking of Toy, don't you relieve him about now?"

"Soon as I coffee up." Boulders disappeared up to the galley and Clint headed out to the main deck and a scuttlebutt of water to wash down with.

He was polished up as best he could in the short time when he made his way down the gangplank and up to Hutchinson's office. As usual, Horace Griswold, the clerk, kept him waiting in the outer office, but he wasn't the only one waiting. Joshua, Hutchinson's big black slave, sat across the small room. He nodded in friendly recognition of Clint, but said nothing.

After twenty minutes the door opened. Clint jumped to his feet, as did Joshua. Rachel DuBois, looking even more beautiful than the first time he'd seen her, in a yellow gown and yellow Jenny Lind parasol, strolled out.

"Why, Mr. Ryan, I wondered what had happened to you."

"Miss DuBois." Clint pulled the fawn-colored hat off his head.

"Cut the formalities," Hutchinson called from deep in the office. "We've got work."

"My, he's a grump this morning," she said, giving Clint a smile that melted even his irritation at Hutchinson's manner. "I'd like to chat with you sometime today, Mr. Ryan, about the problems of singing to a group of rowdy men . . . if you don't mind."

"At your pleasure, ma'am," Clint said. Then Garth Hutchinson's large frame filled the doorway between the anteroom and his private office.

"No, Ryan, at *my* pleasure." He glared at the two, his brow furrowed. "Can we get on with this?"

"I'm off to the city," Rachel said, leading Joshua out the door.

Clint followed Hutchinson into the office, and remained standing as the other man took his chair behind the desk and didn't bother to offer him one.

"I trust you've finished your other business and can get to work?" Hutchinson groused.

"I can get to work."

"Then your pay starts now. We've got problems."

"I heard about the cut in fares."

"That is a devious—no, a heinous act, meant to ruin this boat."

"Looks like they cut the fares down to about break even, with the take from the gambling and the food," Clint said, guessing at what it took to run the ship.

Hutchinson pondered that a moment, then rose and began to pace with his hands folded behind his back. His tone mellowed, like a preacher lecturing the congregation.

"It'll cost a lot of jobs, good men's jobs, if this boat doesn't run. Men whose families will starve without income. And a whole lot of good folks will eventually end up paying a lot more for transportation without the competition. All of California will suffer and her economy will be seriously damaged. We have a moral obligation to see that that doesn't happen."

Clint listened with interest—and amazement. Hutchinson spoke as if Clint didn't know that there were more jobs in California than men to fill them. Hutchinson could be a real chameleon. He should have been a politician or a preacher, Clint decided.

Suddenly Hutchinson stopped pacing, turned, and placed a hand on Clint's shoulder. The friendliness of the gesture surprised Clint. "You do value this job, don't you, Clint?"

"Under the circumstances," Clint almost mumbled, not quite forgetting that Hutchinson had coerced him aboard.

"Then you've got to be a real master-at-arms, a true friend to the *Belle* and myself."

"That's what I'm paid to do," Clint said. He was beginning to wonder what Hutchinson was driving at.

Garth Hutchinson turned and walked to the window, his hands again folded behind his back. He stared out it at the *Belle,* tied alongside the dock below, as he spoke. "The *Belle* is a boon to all California. It would be a sin against California—against God Himself—if she were not able to do her calling."

My God, Clint thought, *that's taking it a little far. After all, she's only timber and cast iron, even if trimmed in silk and crystal, hardly a deity.*

Hutchinson turned and looked Clint straight in the eye. "You've got to sink the *River Ruler.*" He said it as if he were sending Clint to the galley to fetch him a cup of coffee.

Clint studied him a moment to see if the man were jesting, then the heat started to creep up his spine. He wanted to shout that he was just about to get out of the shadow of one warrant for his arrest, and he was not about to do *anything* to create another —specially something that would cost many innocent lives.

"I'm being paid to protect the *Belle*, Hutchinson, not to destroy other people's property."

At those words, Hutchinson smiled, but somehow it looked more like a smirk to Clint. He turned away, then cleared his throat. "I didn't mean literally, Ryan. You do your job, and we'll sink her . . . financially."

"Oh," Clint said, sure the man was covering his real intent.

"Of course," Hutchinson said, staring out the window again, "it would be worth thousands to us if she did go to the bottom, with a couple of hundred men aboard. That would seal the fate of the California Steam Navigation Company."

Clint stood silently, waiting to see just how far Hutchinson would go. There was a long pause.

"We still sail on Friday?" Clint finally asked, purposefully changing the subject.

Hutchinson spun away from the window,

his eyes full of fire, his look no longer that of the benevolent preacher. "Yes, and you damned well better be ready. I want no trouble aboard the *Belle*. More importantly at the moment, we've invited San Francisco's elite for a trial run around the harbor day after tomorrow. We're putting on the dog with lunch and entertainment. I want no problems."

"I'll be ready, for Thursday and for the maiden voyage on Friday," Clint said, his jaw beginning to clench at Hutchinson's condescending tone.

"See that you are. You're excused," Hutchinson snapped, and turned back to the window, rocking back on his heels.

Clint headed for the door.

"By the way, Ryan!" Clint paused as he reached for the knob. "That's the second time you've called me Hutchinson—without the mister. You do it again and I'll rescind that bond and you'll find yourself waiting for that inquest in jail." His tone began to take on a triumphant air. "And that inquest might just determine that you have to stand trial for murder—"

"Attempted murder and assault," Clint corrected, without turning.

"Then you won't need this job or any

other," Hutchinson continued as if he didn't hear him.

Clint turned the knob and started out the door without replying.

"And Ryan, you best remember that I'm a key—no, *the* key witness in your defense. No one will pay any mind to what Joshua might say in court. Besides, he'll say whatever I tell him to say. You wouldn't want me to be unhappy. Even attempted murder will get you several years in this state, and her new judges, and prosecutors are dying to make a name for themselves.

Clint paused halfway out the door, listening without turning, as Hutchinson continued, his tone low, as if speaking through clenched teeth.

"Maybe you better reconsider how much you owe to the *Belle*."

Clint slammed the door behind him. He caught a glance from a well-dressed man who waited in the anteroom as he stomped by Griswold's desk.

After he had left, the clerk went to the connecting door and opened it. "Mr. Hutchinson. Mr. Roderick from Scarsdale, Roderick, and St. Clair is here about the insurance,"

Clint climbed the gangplank at a brisk

stride. He had never wanted to whip a man more than he wanted to whip Garth Hutchinson at the moment. But the last thing he needed now was to lose one more hour in jail. San Francisco was a caldron of honest citizens, who would use any means to clean up the streets, and the dishonest ones, who fought to rule them. Sam Brannan and his vigilantes were currently ruling the streets, and a man could be hanged on suspicion. It was no time to come to trial in the city, innocent or not. And Clint had to find the retainer for Stanhope, had to find someone to go to Don Carlos and get a list of men to take depositions from, and had to stay on board the *Belle* so Hutchinson didn't pull the bond and get him thrown back into jail for attempted murder and assault. And Hutchinson was just the kind of son of a bitch who would refuse to testify truthfully —if he had an ax to grind. It galled Clint to remember that just the night before he was worried about the man, and about the allegiance he owed him for the job. He must have been more tired than he thought after the long ride. Still, Clint decided as he began to calm down, he had to be careful as a naked man climbing over a thorn-bush hedge. In a heartbeat, he could get in a world of hurt. But it galled and frustrated him—he felt like a stump-tailed horse in fly time.

He decided seeing Rachel DuBois might calm his nerves, and headed straight for her cabin, then remembered that she was going to town with Joshua. He would see her later. Instead, he sought out Boulders Blanchard, who was pacing the deck, on watch.

Clint walked up beside him. "Boulders, I need a favor."

"Ask."

"You've got to head back to Rio Ancho and take a message to Don Carlos for me."

Within the hour, Blanchard was on his way with a carefully penned message, and Clint had awakened Toy to take the day watch. Toy, as usual, did not question the fact that he had only had two hours of sleep, just went to the job uncomplaining. Clint left the boat, headed back to Stanhope's office, and as was beginning to seem his fate, was kept waiting in the man's anteroom. Finally the blond clerk showed him in.

"You have my retainer?" Stanhope asked, his round face framed by his great gray sideburns and backlit by a tall window looking over Montgomery Street. He looked up from the paperwork on his wide desk.

166

"No, but I've got a proposition for you."

"I've got about five minutes, propose away."

"Horses are bringing fifty dollars a head. How about I bring you five head of prime Andalusian horseflesh from Rancho del Rio Ancho—"

"Horses eat, then you've got to shovel up what it cost you to feed them. That makes them double trouble, and a damned bad investment, Mr. Ryan. Cash is the king."

Clint was taken aback. Horses made the world go round, at least in California.

"You can sell them."

"Then you sell them and bring me the money."

"How about a matched set, and I mean identical, of dappled grays, trained to the harness, gaited, high-steppin', and long-maned and -tailed? The finest in California." Clint winced as he said it, wondering how Don Carlos would feel about Clint trading away his beautiful carriage team.

Stanhope seemed to weaken.

"I'm sure a man like you has the finest of buggies," Clint added, appealing to the man's vanity.

Stanhope puffed like a peacock strutting in front of a flock of peahens. "Actually, I've just ordered a fine calèche from the East Coast. It won't be here for another four months, however. No sense in feeding a team until it arrives."

"We'll keep them on Rio Ancho until you call for their delivery. You can send your coachman there—"

"Five head of Andalusians and the team of gray's," Stanhope said without looking up from his paperwork.

"How much over the two-hundred-dollar retainer might this matter run?" Clint asked.

"Might go as much as four hundred."

"Then five head of Andalusians and the grays, we feed them all until you sell them or call for them, up to a year, say, and we get four hundred dollars' credit."

"Three hundred," Stanhope said, still not looking up.

"Three fifty, and six months' feed and care on us."

"Done," Stanhope said, arose, and shook hands with Clint, then sat back to his paperwork. "Robert Miles here will help with the depositions. Let him know when you're ready."

"I'll need him to go to Sonora, to Sacramento, and finally to Monterey."

Stanhope looked up, and seemed to be figuring a second. "Then the fee will probably be closer to six hundred."

"Six hundred?" Clint moaned.

"Closer to six hundred, one side or the other."

Clint sighed deeply. "Six hundred," he stated resignedly.

He turned and started for the door as Stanhope looked up again. "And Mr. Ryan, I don't need any donkeys or mules or goats or chickens."

"I know, Mr. Stanhope, cash is king."

Stanhope glanced up, but Clint had already closed the door. *Damn,* he thought, *I should have made him throw in some harness.*

Clint went straight to Bamber Express, which had new service to Monterey via a fine Concord coach, addressed a cover to Captain Quade Sharpentier, and on a single page informed him that he could have his attorney submit the statement and agreement to Stanhope for his perusal. He sealed it and passed his next-to-last dollar over the counter to the agent for the delivery. As he walked out of the office Clint smiled wryly, thinking that for his last two dollars he could have gotten a much larger envelope—but he didn't have a rattler to put in it anyway. Still, the thought warmed him.

Clint was back on the *Belle* an hour after he had left, and again went to Rachel DuBois's cabin. This time she was there.

"Come in," she said, her emerald eyes sparkling. She had removed the yellow dress and stood clad in a floor-length silk wrap, her hair pulled back and staked with a jeweled comb. "I was hoping you would stop by."

Clint entered, leaving the door ajar, as a gentleman would.

"Push the door shut," she said softly, and he did so.

"Brandy?" she asked. She crossed the plush room to a sideboard, opened it, removed two glasses, and poured them both a drink without awaiting his answer.

"Thank you," Clint said, hardly able to keep his eyes off the way the silk clung to the curves of her body then swirled away as she moved. He caught the look of amusement in her eyes at the way he watched her.

"Sit," she said, more of a command than a request. He took a seat at a small table, and she sat across from him.

"To the success of the *Belle*." She offered her glass to touch his, and he did. As they each sipped she seemed to appraise him. "I asked you here to talk about the problems of security, but since then I've had another chance to speak to Garth. Seems we are in a great deal of trouble."

"We, or Garth Hutchinson?" Clint asked a little coldly.

"The *Belle*, Mr. Ryan, the *Belle*, and after all, you make your living here just as the rest of us do . . . don't you?" For the first time since he had met her, her tone turned cold.

"You could say that," he said, without explaining that he had been coerced into the job.

"In fact, Garth tells me you owe him a great deal."

Clint made a couple of false starts before he got his tongue on track, and it was a good thing he did, for he really didn't want to say what had immediately come to mind. Instead, he arose. "Are we going to talk about your security? If not, I've got work to do.

"Just relax," she said, her voice once more smooth as silk and twice as seductive. "We can talk about the problem of my safety, then I want to hear all about you."

"I'm a short story," he said, his voice still strained.

"Then let's talk about what you're going to do to ensure my safety, Mr. Ryan." She smiled brilliantly, her cold tone gone completely, then crossed her legs and showed a bit of ankle. As much as he tried, Clint could not keep his eyes from drifting down.

This is a woman used to getting exactly what she wants, he thought as she talked of problems she had had while singing in front of a crowd of rowdy men. As she continued, occasionally smiling and batting her eyes, Clint caught the scent of whatever perfume she wore and found himself thinking, for the hundredth time since he had ridden away from Rio Ancho, about the night he spent with Apolonia Vega. Apolo-nia had nowhere near this woman's sophistication, but her simplicity, and honesty, and the heat of her touch kept bringing his thoughts back to her.

"Are you distracted?" Rachel DuBois suddenly asked, apparently not used to men not giving her their undivided attention.

"No, no, just a lot on my mind. Master-at-arms is a big responsibility."

After they had talked for a half hour, Clint arose with the excuse that he had to get back to his job. As he made his way to

172

the door, over her complaints, she arose and crossed the room. Coyly placing her hand on his chest, she looked up at him. Those eyes could have heated the *Belle*'s big boilers.

"If something happened to the *River Ruler*," she cooed, suddenly changing the subject and her attitude as she got close enough so her scent filled his nostrils, "then all of our jobs would be assured, and the success of the *Belle* would be a great thing for all of California."

Clint stepped back away from her, and she almost lost her balance with his sudden move. "You sound a little like Garth Hutchinson," he snapped.

Her eyes turned cold again. "If I do, then we both make sense. I'm taking his money, and I plan to do my job."

"And I plan to do mine," Clint said evenly.

She suddenly smiled. "You do?"

"I do."

"That's wonderful, Clint," she said, using his first name for the first time. "I would be forever in your debt if you did. Then all of our troubles would be over." The top of her gown opened slightly, exposing ample cleavage, and resist as Clint might, his eyes drifted down. They both knew she had achieved another little victory.

Clint nodded and left, knowing she misunderstood his intent, and not giving a damn if she did. That was his little victory. She had heard what remained unsaid—what she wanted to hear. One thing he had learned, it was hard to put a foot in a shut mouth.

Besides, the less he said now, the more time he had to solve his problems. His problems were balls in the air, and he felt like a circus juggler.

"Goddamn, man," a voice rang behind him, grating his backbone like a rasp file. Clint turned to see Garth Hutchinson stomping up. "Every time I go looking for you, you're somewhere else. The next time you decide to leave this vessel, you get my permission."

"Yes, sir, Mr. Hutchinson," Clint said through clenched teeth. He decided as he walked away that those were the hardest four words he'd ever managed to spit out.

8

Clint spent most of the next day studying the boat.

He and Toy took turns with the watch. Boulders arrived that evening, a little drunk from partaking of the *River Ruler's* good whiskey on the way from Benicia and feeling his oats, as usual, but right on time. Clint gave Toy a few hours shore leave so he could attend a tong meeting, and it was a good thing he did, for he came straight to Clint on his return.

"Sydney Ducks take great interest in festivities on *Belle*," he said, his deep voice rumbling.

"What do you mean, Toy?" Clint asked.

"Free food and whiskey is all the talk on Barbary Coast. It is said there will be many bulging pockets to pick. We need watch for them."

"Just that? No other mischief you heard

about?" Clint was far more worried about serious attempts on the boat's safety.

"Just that. But there many Sydney Ducks, many plan slip aboard."

The next morning, Clint spent several hours with Toy and Boulders, going over the following day's activities, and called a special meeting of the roustabouts and engine crew, including even the full-time waiters and bartenders. He, Toy, and Boulders took short four-hour shifts that night so each man would get his share of rest.

The *Belle* was a buzz of activity on Thursday morning. Vendors from all over San Francisco and the bay area crowded the docks with drays and pushcarts, and pulled alongside in fishing vessels. Oysters, crabs, abalones, petrole sole, fruit, vegetables, sides of beef and whole lambs and pigs, kegs of beer and wine, and cases of whiskey and liquors were loaded aboard. A full twelve-piece orchestra crowded up the gangplank with their array of instruments. Rachel DuBois stayed busy directing a crew of men who strung brilliantly colored ribbons from the boat's rails, balustrades, and cable stays. The Belle looked like a carnival boat by noon.

Henry Slocumb, the pilot, was at his repulsive best, Clint thought as the man hurried about getting in everyone's way and expressing his opinion on every small item. He reigned resplendent in white coat and blue trousers with a yellow stripe down the leg matching his yellow cravat. His blue pilot's hat gleamed in the sunlight, trimmed in gold braid as if he were a commodore aboard a U.S. frigate. He attempted to tell Clint what to do, but Clint sidestepped and frustrated him by saying he was already doing Hutchinson's bidding.

Even the gulls and pelicans seemed to respect the *Belle's* coming-out, circling her and crying their raucous screams in salute but not alighting or soiling her. Two of the city's drum-and-bugle corps, each a half-dozen strong, uniformed, representing a fire brigade and the Masonic lodge, crowded aboard and added to the bedlam. Cooks from three of the city's finest hotels and a Chinese chef who had gained an instant reputation in the city for his exotic dishes had been hired for the day, much to the chagrin of the disgruntled permanent cook of the *Belle*.

It had dawned on Clint that if Garth Hutchinson was thinking about trying to sink the *River Ruler,* then there was a good possibility the California Steam Navigation Company had a similar thought, and the *Belle* would be in imminent danger.

Clint and the boys had their hands full, going from place to place, checking every conceivable container for black powder that could cause enough of an explosion to hole the *Belle*'s thick hide. No spot was left unturned, even cornet cases and iced oyster crates were rifled through, over the complaints of musicians and vendors.

Finally, just before noon, the crowd began to arrive, and the drum-and-bugle corps alternated lively marches to pipe them aboard.

In buggies and hansom cabs, horseback and afoot, they were deposited at the boat's festooned gangplank, each dressed in his or her best for the occasion—though the *hers* were almost exclusively Mexican doñas, and even those were few. Clint recognized the city marshal, with his broad-brimmed white hat, as he boarded with some other dignitaries. Garth Hutchinson stayed near the foot of the gangplank, since each guest was expected to bring his fine engraved parchment invitation in order to be allowed aboard. Clint stood back near the head of the plank, his arms crossed across his chest, his Navy' Colt's displayed on his hip, a small brass shield identifying him as the boat's master-at-arms pinned on his shirt.

Clint kept a close eye on the growing crowd and began to notice an increase in the riffraff pressing closer to the gangplank. He recognized a number of Sydney Ducks with their prominent mustaches among the growing thong on the dock. Crossing to the engine room, he pulled open the door and went to the voice pipe that communicated up to the pilot's house and pulled the bell string.

"Slocumb," the answering voice echoed.

"Ryan, Mr. Slocumb. Stand by to give a long and two shorts on the whistle."

"I'm busy up here, Ryan. I've got a boat to run,"

"And we're busy down here, Big Henry, but if you want to show off this boat, you'll do as I ask. I'll go take Hutchinson away from his guests if you want it from the lion's mouth." Clint had to shout louder than usual into the tube to make himself heard.

There was a short pause. "A long and two shorts. Now or do you want me to stand here with my ear pressed to this damned pipe?"

"No. When you hear three pulls on the bell, jump to it."

"Fine, Ryan, but this had better be important."

Clint had an engine wiper, the lowest among the employees in the engine room, stand by the engine-room door to watch for his signal, then took his place back by the gangplank.

As he suspected, the Ducks were gathering up, one group of twenty or so each side of the gangplank. Clint tried to catch Hutchinson's attention at the foot of the gangplank, but the man was too busy glad-handing the guests to look up.

Clint watched carefully, and as soon as Hutchinson stepped away from his position to greet some special guest, a half dozen of the Ducks elbowed into line and began the forty-foot ascent up the angled plank. Clint gave the high sign to the boy at the voice-pipe bell. The boy stepped out of sight into the engine room, and almost immediately, the boat's whistle sounded a long and two shorts. By the time the group of burly and roughly dressed Ducks reached the top of the gangplank, waiters and bartenders were descending the stairways from the salon above, and roustabouts were gathering behind Clint. Clint was surprised when Stubby O'Flarraty came on the run, one of the first of the crew to arrive. He carried a polished shillelagh he must have kept hidden in his desk.

"We've got this handled," Clint said quietly as Stubby moved up to back his play.

"You'll not be leavin' me out of the fun, Clint Ryan," Stubby growled, obviously irritated that he had not been invited to Clint's meeting.

Clint knew the man leading the first group of interlopers aboard. Farley Tucker had a reputation on the Barbary Coast for taking what he wanted, and using any means to get it. Taller than Clint, he was long of limb and whipcord tough, and carried a scar across one eye that meandered down his cheek. The eye had withered and been replaced by a painted wooden ball. Clint assumed he was armed. Even though no weapons were in sight, he wore a coat he could have concealed a fire ax beneath.

The last thing Clint wanted was trouble, with distinguished guests moving in front and behind the approaching Ducks and crowding the decks and docks below.

Clint faced Farley Tucker as soon as the laughing man topped the gangplank.

"Tucker, isn't it?" Clint asked in a friendly tone, and Farley stopped laughing. His eyes cut down to the shield on Clint's chest.

"Tucker it is, mate. You some kinda river-boat bobby?"

"That's close enough. I'm the law aboard the *Belle*. You boys got your look at the boat, now how about turning around and working your way back down that gang-plank?"

Tucker turned back casually and studied the plank, crowded four wide and forty deep with guests, and at another group of a half-dozen Ducks who had crowded in line.

"Seems a mite difficult task, mate. No way could a body get back through that herd. Why don't you jus' stand aside an' let us good fellas take a gander at your fine floatin' palace?"

"You're welcome back sometime, Tucker. But *this* party is invitation only. Sorry, but it's back down the plank for you and your boys here."

"Welcome back when it costs, ya mean, mate. Now, I think that's downright un-neighborly. Somethin' the rest of these blokes got that we don't?"

"Yeah," Clint said without hesitation.

"An invitation for one thing, and good manners for another."

Tucker had stalled long enough that the second group of Ducks were aboard, and Clint glanced down to see that another half dozen were on the plank. He had to act.

He turned to the group of men who had begun to form around the Ducks and gave his best ship's captain imitation: "Gentlemen, repel boarders!"

The bartenders, waiters, and roustabouts began to close in a circle around the Ducks, forcing the two groups together, shouldering the elegantly garbed guests out of the potential melee—smiling all the time, but moving side by side and acting as if the crowd behind were forcing them. One of the Ducks pushed away, thinking he might get lost in the crowd, but Stubby drove the shillelagh deep into his gut in a move so quick the guests hardly noticed, and two of the crew caught the man under the arms before he folded to his knees. They had all twelve Ducks in a knot against the rail in just a few seconds.

Toy and Boulders stood at Clint's side, and two dozen men backed him up.

Tucker stood red in the face and snarling

when he realized he had been bested. "Each of my boys is worth a dozen of you."

"Could be," Clint said. "But you and your boys should have taken my suggestion and made your way back down the plank."

"Up yours, mate," Farley Tucker said, and his hand snaked inside his wrinkled coat.

Clint stepped in and locked the man's wrists in an iron grip. His face was six inches from Farley's, and he spoke very quietly. "Farley, whatever you've got under that coat better stay there, or I guarantee I'll use your greasy hide to fire the *Belle*'s boilers."

"We're aboard mate," Tucker snarled, his fetid breath in Clint's face. "We can't get back down your bloody plank, so just let us be."

"You're getting off this boat."

"And just how the hell do you expect us—"

"Show him, Toy," Clint said over his shoulder, not taking his eyes off Farley.

Toy reached out and encircled two of the other Ducks' collars in his thick dark hands, and while the men kicked and swung at him he hoisted them up with their feet dangling and shoved his way to the rail. Unceremoniously, like garbage, he dropped them overboard. Their screaming profanities were cut short as they disappeared into the ten-foot space between the *Belle* and the dock, then beneath the flotsam-covered water.

"You son of a bitch!" Farley yelled in Clint's face. He tried to head-butt him, since his hands were held tightly, but Clint dodged. Before Clint could intervene, the man was knocked stupid with a crashing right hook from Boulders, who caught his sagging frame as Clint let him go and hoisted him over a shoulder like a sack of flour then deposited him over the side. Some of the Ducks jumped over before the rest of the crew charged, and some had to be thrown over. A few of the last group to reach the deck tried to blend into the crowd, but were quickly found and dumped into the bay from the closest rail. The skirmish was over almost before the guests realized something was happening.

"Damn," Boulders said, siding up to Clint after it quieted. "I had hopes those boys had more spunk. We could have had us a real Donnybrook Fair, an' I'm way overdue."

"Old Farley was unconscious when you

dropped him over. I hope he came to," Clint said, concerned for the man even though he had been in the wrong.

"Hell, he probably couldn't swim anyways, Boulders said with a satisfied smirk.

Clint shouldered his way to the rail amid the laughing crew and looked over. Some of the Ducks, including Farley, were clinging to the pilings under the plank wharf. A few were being tossed lines by those that had remained on the dock, but most had made their way to a ladder and were climbing up on the wharf, where a number of San Francisco's city marshals were busily moving them along. Clint sent Toy and Boulders down to the dock to make sure the marshals did their job and the Ducks continued on their way, then continued his deck watch.

He was glad he had the foresight to call the meeting and work out a signal for the rest of the crew. Even with Toy and Boulders, the three of them could not have begun to handle a baker's dozen of tough Sydney Ducks. Of course, they had had Stubby's help.

They continued to patrol the boat.

Clint remained all business, until a wide smile crossed his face. To his great surprise,

Apolonia Vega, on her father's arm, arrived on board among a group of other dons and doñas from the outlying ranchos. She pulled away from her father, her beautiful lace-trimmed turquoise gown swirling around her, and moved to greet him.

He took her hand, brushing his lips across her warm fingers. "I'm glad you're here," he began, "I had no idea—"

"Mr. Hutchinson invited many of us who might have freight to ship on the *Belle* . . . and of course he and my father are involved in the wood yard."

"I wish I wasn't working," Clint said, a little regretfully.

"I should caution you that Father wants to discuss that very matter with you . . . your working here. And we have heard of some of your trouble."

"Thanks for the warning," Clint said with a smile.

"Will you have any time off?" she asked coyly. The look in her dark eyes grew even warmer.

"Not today," he answered, with obvious disappointment. "How long will you be in San Francisco?" But before Apolonia could answer, Don Carlos crossed the deck and nodded to him, a grave look on his face.

"Lazo!" The old man's lined face looked worried as he shook hands with little enthusiasm. "I sent Sancho to meet with this *abogado*, Stanhope, and to take his man out to the ranchos to gain the testimony. *Madre de Dio*, aren't there many other things you should be doing to help us with our problem?"

"Not until the depositions arrive, Don Carlos."

"A few of the dons are here today for this festive occasion and many have already gone to Mr. Stanhope's office for their statements."

"Good, that will save us money."

"Money? You have traded my finest team and live good Andalusians away."

Clint felt his face flush. "I'm sorry. If I'd enough gold with me, it would not have been necessary. I'll pay you for them if you wish."

Don Carlos's face softened. "It is of little matter. Just save Rancho del Rio Ancho." The old don cleared his throat before he continued, his tone hard again. "Tell me, Lazo, why do I need to hire you for this task if I am using an expensive *abogado* and his staff to accomplish the same purpose?"

Apolonia quickly excused herself, not

188

wanting to overhear what she suspected would be a confrontation between her father and Clint Ryan. She rejoined some of the other women.

"You said get the job done, Don Carlos, and that's what I'm doing. The attorney will guarantee that it's done right. I have ridden to Monterey and obtained the advice and cooperation of Edward Fitzgerald Beale to plead your case to the Land Commission. We're doing exactly what he advises. I have my own problems here in San Francisco that must be attended to if I'm going to be able to help you."

The old don shook his head, worry resting on his shoulders. "I have already done as I promised. Two dozen horses and two vaqueros are on their way to your Kaweah Rancho. But you, .Lazo . . . Can you help me, with so many personal problems and other interests?" He cut his eyes to Apolonia, who stood talking with some other colorfully gowned women.

Clint dreaded what was coming, but the don made no mention of his daughter as he continued.

"I have heard of your arrest. This is disturbing. And working for the *Belle* seems a strange way to help the Vegas."

"True enough. But I have no choice. Results are what counts, and if the Vegas' title can be protected, we are doing all we can to do so."

"I hope so, Lazo." There was a long silence as the two men locked eyes.

Clint was tempted to tell him that he had not wanted this responsibility in the first place, that all he wanted was to be back at the Kaweah, but he didn't.

Apolonia walked back beside Clint and took his arm, smiling up at him, and Don Carlos frowned even more deeply.

"I hope we will see you—" she began.

"We must rejoin the others," Don Carlos interrupted. He took his daughter's hand and led her away from Clint's side.

She looked over her shoulder and flashed him a last smile as she followed her father across the increasingly crowded deck. Clint wondered if Don Carlos was only concerned about his working on board the *Belle* instead of attending to the Vegas' title problem. Surely Sancho Guiterrez had said nothing to the old man about Clint's indiscretion . . . if Sancho even knew.

Clint sighed deeply, then went back to his business.

Soon the *Belle* cast off to the whistles and

bells of the other boats and ships in the harbor, and the continuing bleat of her own piercing two-toned steam whistle. As soon as she began to pull away from the dock, Hutchinson hurried to Clint's side.

"I've got something very important for you to do, Clint," he said, suddenly friendly. "Those three gentlemen"—he pointed to three men in city coats and tophats—"require a tour of the boat. A detailed tour. Make damn sure they know she's the safest boat ever built."

"She is safe," Clint said.

"Make damn sure they know it. Come on." He led Clint to the men's side and introduced him to Mr. Scarsdale, Mr. Roderick, and Mr. St. Clair. Clint realized he had seen Roderick in Hutchinson's anteroom. Something to do with insurance. Clint gave them the full tour.

And the *Belle* performed beautifully, stopping just as she pulled away from the dock to reverse one of her wheels and spin a three-hundred-and-sixty-degree circle in her own length, to the amazement of the passengers, and to the interest of the press, who were busily taking notes and following Garth Hutchinson wherever he led.

Before the circle was complete, Garth

amazed them again by having the canvas cover of the calliope pulled away to reveal the St. Louis musician seated in top hat and tails, and in an instant steam puffed out of her brass pipes and the clarion tones of the instrument began to serenade the passengers and the dockful of onlookers with "Hail Columbia." The crowd roared ecstatically and hats sailed into the air.

Before he was a quarter mile from the docks, Garth Hutchinson had won the day.

The trip was uneventful so far as Clint was concerned. Scarsdale, Roderick, and St. Clair were properly impressed and confided in Clint that they would write the quarter million-dollar policy insuring the *Belle*. Clint knew little about such matters, but did recognize the name of their associates across the Atlantic—Lloyd's of London. They wrote far more ship insurance than any other company in the world. Hutchinson always went for the best, and usually got it.

Rachel DuBois sought Clint out and took his arm, laughing a little too loudly and flashing her beautiful emerald eyes, when it was time to move the crowd into the main salon where she was scheduled to sing and where Garth Hutchinson hoped to get the crowd gambling and get some of his money back. Clint caught Apolonia's hurt look as he escorted Rachel into the salon, where the doñas and their daughters would never go, even if allowed.

As they moved through the crowd Rachel rose up on her tiptoes to whisper in his ear. "I thought the *River Ruler* was going to sink this week?"

"Was she?" Clint said innocently, and winked at her.

Satisfied, she said nothing more, but moved through the throng laughing and smiling, and inviting the crowd into the salon to hear her sing.

Clint looked back and realized Apolonia had been watching Rachel whisper in his ear and had seen the emerald-eyed beauty place a hand on the back of his neck. Apolonia looked crushed and turned away quickly and followed the other doñas.

Hutchinson had opened the women's parlor. Most of the women retired there, including Apolonia, where he had tea and a string quartet for their pleasure. He had thought of everything. Clint watched them go, thinking that he would come back and speak to her after he got Rachel to the stage, but he couldn't. The ladies' parlor was off limits even to the master-at-arms, unless the most severe emergency arose.

At Hutchinson's orders, in the center of the bay, one of the crew "fell" overboard as the Belle was making a brisk fourteen knots. The crowd screamed and crowded to the rails. Henry Slocumb, with Garth Hutchinson looking over his shoulder, reversed the engines then threw one into forward, as they had rehearsed, to properly angle the boat to pick the man up. They fished him out with a boat hook only four minutes after he went in. He was an excellent swimmer, but the press still ate it up—and Henry Slocumb basked in the praise of all aboard.

Everything went off as planned and the celebrants were deposited back on the dock, full of exotic food and liquor, just as the sun set. Clint was pleased with the lack of problems but disappointed that Don Carlos seemed determined to keep a close eye on his daughter and to keep her away from him. Finally Apolonia managed, in passing, to answer his question about how long she would be in San Francisco, though in doing so she seemed much cooler than she had when she'd first arrived. She and her father were to be Garth Hutchinson's guests on the *Belle*'s maiden voyage to Sacramento, and they were spending the night in one of the boat's private cabins.

Clint was not invited to dine in the private dining room where the overnight guests were served, and could find no excuse to make an appearance. He waited on the deck, hoping Apolonia would take an evening stroll with her father, but she did not. He did not see her until the next morning, and only then as she strolled the decks on her father's arm. His only attempt at a conversation was cut short by the sullen don.

The *Belle* sailed for Sacramento at 9:00 A.M., right on time, but her decks were surprisingly empty of passengers. Only at the last minute had Garth Hutchinson relented and lowered her prices to match those of the *River Ruler*, and by then it had been too late. He had hoped that the press and the lure of the magnificent new boat would attract travelers even if they had to pay more, and the morning *San Francisco Call* had sung his boats praises, calling her the safest and most luxurious afloat. It was a ploy that had no effect on the eager passengers, however; transportation was what they wanted, and the cheaper and quicker the better.

A longer-than-normal stop in Benicia allowed its prominent citizens to board the *Belle* for free drinks and lunch.

As they churned past the wood yard Clint watched intently, satisfied with the progress of the work on the wharf, which appeared to be finished as scheduled; a twenty-foot-high-by-twenty-foot-wide mound of cordwood stretched over a hundred paces along the shore of Honker Bay.

Not long after passing Honker, Clint leaned on the nearside rail, surprised to see the frame of a church rising on the riverbank—on a portion of Rancho del Rio Ancho's riverbank. The preacher Moses McClanahan and a crew of a half dozen, all dressed in black, worked diligently as the *Belle* passed, not even glancing up at the new queen of the river. Clint was even more surprised at the row of signs placed along the bank. REPENT, THE GREAT EARTHQUAKE IS COMING. GOD'S WRATH WILL FALL ON THOSE WHO SIN. The signs went on for a quarter of a mile with a wide variety of admonitions, which to Clint seemed a larger project than the building of the Church of the River Redeemer. Clint had heard the rivermen talking about Moses while he was still in San Francisco, and

196

Moses was now being called the Prophet, as he had proclaimed himself to be. Clint chuckled as they passed and wondered if the gaunt man was considered a prophet in his own land, wherever that may be. He had heard it said that you had better not say a thing unless you wanted it to happen. Maybe that was coming true for Moses.

Apolonia Vega disembarked at Sacramento's waterfront in the late afternoon, able only to wave at Clint, who was busy overseeing the off- and on-loading of supplies and checking them for explosives. Don Carlos Vega glanced in Clint's direction, but did not acknowledge the tipping of Clint's hat in farewell.

The *Belle*'s workday was far from over, and as she had in San Francisco, she entertained the elite of Sacramento at supper that night.

Finally, at almost midnight, work stopped. Toy had the deck duty, so Clint and Boulders went ashore to get away from the boat for a while. They bought a quart of cheap but potent *pulque* and decided on a walking tour.

Sacramento City had grown up from the Sacramento River east, just south of the confluence of the American River. She was not the city San Francisco had become, but already she had masonry buildings lining First and Second streets. John Sutter's son, John Jr., had done a good job of laying the city out, being more than happy to accept the five hundred dollars offered for his small city lots—even though they now went for many thousands.

The old fort, farther inland, was also a town center of some importance, with a dozen stores in and around the fort itself. The fort location was much preferred by many, since the riverfront had undergone severe flooding the previous winter. But the river location was just too convenient, and the populace had flooded back as the water receded. Beyond the fort, the *lomerias*—low hills—began climbing until the Sierra rose to grandeur in the distance.

On the embarcadero, along Front Street, and lining First Street a block beyond, lay piles of building and mining materials, most of them covered with old sailcloth, to the embarrassment of the eight hundred ships sitting idle far downriver in San Francisco Harbor. Even in the middle of the night, freighters and muleteers busily loaded freight wagons and packed mule trains, transporting materials to the goldfields.

Like San Francisco, whose waterfront had utilized a number of ships' hulls as buildings, dragging them up out of the water to become saloons and hotels—though many of them had been caught in the fires of the last two years—Sacramento also employed them along the riverbank, albeit to a much lesser extent.

The most prominent of those represented the last hint of civilization north, almost to the mouth of the American. The bark *La Grange* had been stripped of her gear and riveted flat-iron-encased cells added on to her hull; a two-story jail now stood atop her deck. Below, she was still a ship, permanently moored but still afloat, with buttresses flaring out from her hull to support the much wider jail perched atop her, which rose another two stories.

She was a ponderous, and ominous, sight.

Her copper hull sheathing had been used for sieves in gold rockers, her sails for roofs and tents and tarpaulins, her running rigging for lashings for wagons and hoists for the mines, and her galley had been removed in one piece for a much lower purpose—a lawyer's office. This was before her hull had been sold to Sacramento City to be converted to that most necessary of city adornments—a jail.

"That's a dismal sight," Boulders said, and he and Clint turned and started back to the city before they reached the half-ship, half-jail *La Grange,* silhouetted against the brightly starred north sky.

"Not one I'd care to see any closer," Clint agreed.

At the edge of town, they stopped in Round Tent, a saloon named for its shape and walls of sailcloth. Inside, the owners provided only the finest of tables and chairs atop its planked floor, as well as a fine maple back bar and highly polished bar. A bald man playing a pianoforte banged away near the flap that served as a front door, so loud that his melody could almost be heard over the din. They shouldered their way through the crowd and bellied up to the polished maple, ordering a whiskey each.

They downed the three fingers of fire in a gulp, then the burly bartender took umbrage when Boulders pulled the *pulque* bottle out from under the bar and refilled their glasses.

"That won't do in here, fella," the man snapped, carefully staying out of reach of the even more burly, and far more scarred, Boulders Blanchard.

Boulders leaned over the bar and curled a thick finger. "Come over here, son, and I'll do *you* in," he offered with a ghoulish and slightly drunken grin.

Almost before Boulders had finished his offer, the bartender laid an ugly sawed-off scattergun casually across the crook of his arm. "That might be, friend, but odds are ol' Bess here will splatter your green and stinkin' innards all over the customers before you have the chance. An' that would be an embarrassment to the Round Tent."

Never losing his smirk, he ratcheted back both hammers.

9

The bartender smiled, showing a gap, then tapped his remaining front tooth with the stained nail on his thick forefinger. "This here tooth is lonely for his mate, but don't want to join him, and neither does Bess here want him to." He angled the double-barreled scattergun so its two cold eyes stared at Boulders. "So Bess and I'd be obliged if ya'll just make your way outside, peaceablelike."

Boulders removed his narrow-brimmed hat and swung it gallantly across his chest, then bowed deeply, showing the man his bald pate. "I never ignore a lady's request, particular one who can yell as loud as ol' Bess there." He turned and wisely left the saloon. Clint downed his drink then tipped his hat at the man and followed.

He and Boulders sat on a hitching ramp outside until the *pulque* was mostly gone.

Then they continued down Front Street and turned up J Street, which was becoming Sacramento's main east-west thoroughfare. A crowd made its way out of the corner building, the Eagle Theater, one of the city's most impressive structures.

Clint and Boulders came face-to-face with beautiful Rachel DuBois, on the arm of Garth Hutchinson.

Clint pulled his hat off. "Good evening," he slurred slightly.

"You men have to be on the job at six A.M.," Hutchinson snarled.

"You too, Hutchinson," Clint said. "Should Boulders and I escort you two back to the boat so you don't get into any mischief?" He laughed a little too loudly. The boat lay less than forty yards away, its anchor light and gangplank lantern plainly visible.

Hutchinson reddened, but Rachel only flashed one of her brilliant smiles. "Garth is more than capable of taking care of himself and me, thank you, gentlemen."

"I doubt it," Clint mumbled.

"What?" Hutchinson snapped.

"I said, no doubt about it," Clint replied, and Boulders guffawed.

"You two get your carcasses back to the

boat," Hutchinson ordered, his fists clamped at his side.

"My time," Boulders snapped. "Not yours. And I do with my time any damn thing I please."

Clint, too, was beginning to feel the heat on his neck. He had taken just about enough from this man. As Hutchinson sputtered a response Clint added, "Let me tell you something, Hutchinson. You may be the boss on board the *Belle,* but this is the street. I suggest you limit your orders to the boat, and then that you adopt a more genteel manner when you give 'em.

"You never were one of us," Hutchinson said angrily.

"Now, that makes me feel real bad," Clint said, and broke out laughing again.

"You'll both pay for your drunken insubordination," Hutchinson said through clenched teeth.

This time it was Boulders who dragged Clint away, leaving Hutchinson shaking, with Rachel trying to distract him and get him moving in the other direction.

Clint and Boulders walked a half block up J Street before Clint mumbled, "I swear, some men think the sun comes up just to hear them crow."

Boulders guffawed. Then his tone turned serious. "From what you've told me, he's got a big hammer over your head. You better walk careful."

"I just flat don't like the son of a bitch, although to tell the truth, no matter how big an ass he is, he's plowed a hell of a row. I do admire what he's accomplished."

"You two jus' don't sing from the same hymnal." Boulders guffawed loudly again. "C'mon, let's get another drink afore we head back to the boat."

"Yeah, one more drink," Clint agreed, then stumbled along after Boulders. "By the way, what the hell do you know about hymnbooks?'

"There was a time, Clint me boy, when even I was a wee sprout with a mother who applied the Good Book. Usually across my hard noggin, howsomeever," Boulders said with a grin, then turned into another clapboard saloon.

Clint's thoughts had drifted to his parting with Apolonia Vega, and he smiled with self-satisfaction as he remembered her apparent jealousy at seeing him with Rachel DuBois on his arm. Suddenly a feeling bleak as an arctic winter wind swept across him, dousing his fire. It occurred to him that he really didn't want to do anything to make Apolonia Vega unhappy. Brow furrowed in deep thought, he finished his drink in silence, then convinced Boulders to head back to the boat.

The next morning, with head pounding and mouth full of cobwebs, Clint quietly went about his job. Only five passengers boarded the big boat for the return trip, but Clint met the Adam's Express guards at the gangplank—more of them boarding than passengers—and escorted two bags of gold aboard and saw them safely stored in Stubby's big safe. The Adam's boys got their receipt and left. On the trip back to San Francisco one of the guards was always posted at the purser's door, with another on the main deck nearby.

There were even more signs adorning the shore in the vicinity of the Church of the River Redeemer; the church itself had siding in place, and its steeple, though still devoid of a bell, had risen proudly. Clint waved as they steamed by, but the prophet and his disciples were too busy to notice.

They stopped at the wood yard in Honker Bay and took on twenty cords of wood. Chinese and Miwok Indians trudged up the gangplank, loaded with bundles on their backs, while the crew worked the boom on the riverboat's bow and swung great loads aboard. Roustabouts formed a line across the main deck, tossing the three-foot lengths from man to man and stacking them near the boilers, singing a lively work chantey as they did so. Clint moved about on shore while the work continued, looking for a familiar face, but neither Sancho, Don Carlos, nor Apolonia was anywhere to be found.

The *Belle* plowed on to Benicia, then though the Carquinez Straights, across San Pablo Bay, and then the San Francisco Bay without event. After docking, Clint again escorted Adam's Express guards on board after the few passengers had disembarked, and the gold was safely delivered ashore.

Clint did his job and did not confront Garth Hutchinson for the next several days as the *Belle* moved up and down the river. Garth Hutchinson moved about the boat, Passing Clint from time to time but ignoring him. Clint knew things were bad for the *Belle*. She canned few passengers since the California Steam Navigation Company continued to keep prices at rock bottom, and Garth was forced to begin laying off workers. Waiters and kitchen help, half the gamblers, and roustabouts who handled the freight were the first to go. Finally, a week after the *Belle*'s maiden voyage, Clint found it necessary to approach Hutchinson—news had come that the sworn affidavits were ready to be taken to the Land Commission and that Sharpentier's agreement had arrived at Stanhope's office.

He found Hutchinson in the pilothouse shortly after they docked in Sacramento early in the evening. "Can I speak to you a minute?" Clint asked.

Hutchinson, in conversation with Henry Slocumb, glanced over his shoulder. "Wait outside," he said to Clint, his tone cold and aloof.

Clint stepped out of the pilothouse and studied the lanterns and whale-oil lights coming on in the city as he watched, again forcing himself to calm down after being subjected to Garth Hutchinson's demeaning manner.

After a few moments Hutchinson stepped out of the pilothouse. "What's the problem?" he asked brusquely.

"I've got to take a few days off to go to Monterey, starting tomorrow."

Hutchinson's face relaxed and he shook his head, feigning disappointment. Then he seemed to cheer up. "That's just as well, Ryan, considering the lack of business. In fact, it would be helpful to me if you would just resign, if that's not a problem for you."

He must have seen the relief flood Clint's face, for he smiled. "You've done a great job setting up the guard procedures and all that. But Boulders and Toy can more than handle the job from here on out. The problem is, I've asked them to go ashore and help Adam's Express bring a special shipment down from Hangtown. I'll need *you* guarding tomorrow.

Clint was a bit surprised, for Boulders and Toy would normally come to him if someone else ordered them to do something—even Hutchinson or Slocumb. But he shrugged it off, thanking the stars that it looked as if he could finally make a graceful exit from the Belle.

"I've got to get back to San Francisco anyway, and I planned to work through tomorrow night. I only came to you now so you could make arrangements for my absence."

"Good," Hutchinson said, "because Boulders and Toy have to go back to Hangtown, and you'll be the only guard on board on the trip back . . . and I understand it's a big shipment." Again came the friendly laying of a hand on Clint's shoulder, this time followed by a pat or two, like a father encouraging his son, though they were near the same age.

"Come on down to the salon and I'll stand you to a drink in fact, several drinks, for old times' sake," Hutchinson said with a warm smile.

Surprised at Hutchinson's manner and the ease with which he had extracted himself from the boat, but suspicious at the same time, Clint followed him. *Perhaps he'd had thoughts of letting me go anyway,* Clint thought, *things being as they are on the Belle.*

Clint followed him into the salon and straight to the polished cypress bar. Hutchinson slapped it enthusiastically with his flat palm, bringing a bartender running from where he was cleaning tables.

"Get my friend Ryan here anything he wants, and get me a Noble's Finest."

"I'll have the same," Clint said, still amazed at the chameleonic change.

The bartender poured a pair of generous drinks. Hutchinson picked his up and offered it in toast to Clint. "To the best damned master-at-arms a man could ask for."

Clint had no problem drinking to that and touched glasses with him. Immediately, the barman refilled the glasses. "Let me go see if Rachel will join us, Clint. Keep his glass full," Hutchinson commanded, disappearing around the bar to the passageway.

In less than a minute Rachel and he reappeared, and she swished across the floor, dressed only in the silk wrap as she had been when Clint had met with her in her cabin. Her hair was staked up high with a jeweled comb, and this time Clint got a glimpse of the patterned silk stockings she wore on the stage, under lace-up shoes with two-inch heels, as she moved enthusiastically around the end of the bar, her hem swinging.

"I hear you're leaving us," Rachel said, a feigned pout on her lips.

"Duty calls," Clint said, still wary at both their attitudes.

"Let's sit," Hutchinson said, snatching the bottle of fine whiskey off the bar and leading them to a table beside a glass window that overlooked the city. Clint followed obligingly, ushering Rachel with a hand at her back—a hand that discovered that she had little if anything on under the ruffled wrap. Usually, all he felt were whalebone

211

ribs running the wrong way—up and down —when he escorted a fully dressed lady. The warmth of her skin radiated through the silk, heating him all the way to his loins.

He shook off the distraction and turned his attention to Hutchinson. Clint wanted to get a couple of things clear before he departed the boat and decided that now, in front of Rachel, was as good a time as any to broach the problem. Hutchinson was usually in a better mood in the presence of his beautiful hostess.

"My inquest is scheduled on Tuesday of next week. Can I count on you to testify in my behalf?" he asked, looking Garth Hutchinson straight in the eye over their glasses of Nobel's Finest.

"Of course, was there ever any doubt?" Garth said, but his eyes cut away.

"I still owe you a considerable amount of money," Clint said. "I haven't forgotten that."

"I'll take your note. No problem with the bond. I'll be pleased to leave it in place. Just make damn sure you show up," he said, then laughed with uncharacteristic loudness.

"I'll be there," Clint promised.

Rachel gleamed her devastating smile.

"The way Garth and Joshua tell the story, you've got nothing to worry about, Clint."

"Shouldn't have," Clint said, but something was niggling at him, a worm gnawing deep in his gut.

"You two sit here and have a few more drinks. I've got a little more business to take care of," Garth said, and rose, again laying his hand on Clint's shoulder. The worm gnawed even harder.

As soon as Garth Hutchinson moved away from the table, Rachel leaned forward and laid a hand across Clint's. "I had hoped that we would get to be even better friends, Clint," she said, a slight soft smile curving her well-rouged bottom lip. "Now with you leaving . . ."

"I don't have to work here for us to be friends," Clint said, beginning to slip under her spell. He shook it off, knowing he was being suckered.

Hutchinson returned to the table only long enough to have Clint sign the note he had mentioned. Clint would owe him $472 plus interest at the customary eight percent per month, due on demand.

"Still, Ryan, I expect this to be paid."

"Won't they refund your money when I appear as promised?"

"The five hundred, but you'll owe me interest."

"Fair enough," Clint said.

"Good," Hutchinson said. Then he explained how he had to go into Sacramento City on business and wouldn't return until early the next morning. He tucked the note safely into his inside coat pocket and strode out of the salon.

"That leaves the night to us," Rachel said. Her emerald eyes simmered over the top of her upturned glass of whiskey. It was her fourth, and she was beginning to smolder.

Clint wondered if he should, or could, put her fire out. He studied her for a moment, then the worm gnawed again. Suddenly he rose out of the seat.

"I've got some business I've got to take care of, too . . . in town. See you tomorrow."

It would have taken a wagon jack to get Rachel's jaw off her chest as Clint downed his whiskey, spun in his tracks, and strode out of the main salon.

"Son of a bitch," she mumbled under her breath as the barman crossed the room.

"I beg your pardon, Miss Rachel?" he asked.

Rachel rose and stamped her foot, glaring at the barman. "Don't beg, Leon. I hate a man that begs." In a swirl of silk she, too, hurried across the salon floor and disappeared behind the cypress back bar to her cabin.

Leon, the barman, scratched his head and tried to put the short conversation together. Finally, he shrugged his shoulders and wiped the table down. Now he could go on to bed.

He had overheard Clint Ryan say he had to go into Sacramento City and was surprised to see him fast asleep in his bunk in the crew's quarters when he finally finished his cleanup.

Maybe the *Belle* was fated for the success Hutchinson had proclaimed. At sunrise, when Clint headed out of the crew's quarters, passengers were already boarding. One of the deckhands informed him that it had started before midnight, and there had been a continual stream since.

Clint moved down the gangplank, waved a newspaper hawker over, and gave the man a nickel. He got a chuckle when he read the morning *Sacramento Placer*. The headlines proclaimed, PROPHET PREDICTS EARTH-

QUAKE TODAY! The article went on to say that Prophet Moses McClanahan of the Church of the River Redeemer had predicted a major earthquake would rock Sacramento, destroying the caldrons of sin that had grown up in and around the city. opening the earth in great yawning abysses, gaping hot fissures to swallow up the unbelievers who would pour directly into the terrible fires of perdition, and igniting and burning the rest of the city in hell's furious fires. Those who survived God's wrath when the earth shook and swallowed, as a result of His voice raised in anger, would surely perish in the flames.

A few small tremors had been felt in San Francisco, Sacramento, and the gold country over the past months, so the populace took little convincing.

The *Belle* was fast filling with passengers who rushed to escape the impending doom. For the first time since her premaidenvoyage show-off for the citizens of San Francisco, the *Belle* would be packed from rail to rail and stem to stern. Over four hundred crowded aboard, many of them laughing cautiously, making various excuses for needing to go to San Francisco on this particular day, and suggesting and receiving

216

mutual reassurances that surely a boat on the river was the safest place to be in the event of a great quake. After all, the earth would shake, but the river would merely splash around, maybe rocking the boat a little.

Many of the older men aboard confirmed the fact that when the great quakes of the Mississippi River Valley struck in 1807, the safest place to be was on the river.

At eight, after having breakfast with Stubby, who had adopted Clint and had his feelings hurt if he didn't share a cup of coffee with him every day, Clint moved to the dock to await the Adam's Express shipment. The Concord stage arrived right on time, with Toy riding topside with the driver and Boulders inside with one of the usual company guards.

Boulders climbed out of the wagon and helped the guards with one of the four heavy canvas sacks the Concord carried.

It was the biggest shipment so far.

Clint escorted them up the gangplank, and they shouldered through the crowd of passengers to the purser's office, and watched the men heft the bags onto Stubby's scale, then load them into the big safe.

"Must be a hundred and fifty pounds per bag, Clint," Boulders said with a conspiratorial smile on his face as Stubby carefully weighed each bag in. "Makes a fella wish he could tote a bag off for hisse'f."

"Wait till tomorrow, Boulders, if you don't mind. This is my last day on the job."

"Tol' ol' Hutch to sit on his fancy walkin' stick, did ya?"

"Not really. Kind of had a mutual parting of the ways. Actually, he was civil for a change. You should step up and let him know you can handle this master-at-arms job. I'll put a good word in for you."

They walked back to the gangplank, and Clint noticed Garth Hutchinson standing off near the engine room among the crowds of main-deck passengers, carefully monitoring the loading of the shipment and passing the time talking with two rough-looking men as he did so. To Clint's surprise, he recognized one of them as Farley Tucker, the man he had thrown off the *Belle* on her show-off voyage. He made a mental note to keep an eye out for the man.

"There's Hutchinson now," Clint told Boulders. "Why don't you hit him up for the job?"

"What's it pay?"

"Same as yours. I had fifty a week to divvy up. You and I get twenty apiece and Toy gets ten."

"You mean you paid me same as you got?"

"You're worth it, Boulders. So's Toy, but I had to work with what Hutchinson allowed."

"I'll be damned," Boulders said, looking sincerely touched.

"You've already been damned by that ugly mug and uglier disposition of yours." Clint laughed. "Go talk to Hutchinson."

"The hell with Hutchinson. I don't know if I want this lousy job if'n you're a-moving on. Means I'd have to butt heads with that New York dandy every day, and I'd jus' end up buttin' him overboard when he got that sassy tone. Then I'd be a guest at the *La Grange* . . . and jail's somethin' I jus' can't abide."

Clint laughed, sure that Boulders was right. It had been all he could do not to try the same on several occasions.

Boulders' look turned serious. "I don't know why the hell Hutchinson wants Toy and I to head back to Hangtown with these Adam's boys. They won't have another shipment put together for three days.

219

Hell's bells, we'll jus' be cooling our heels there until then."

Clint, too, was puzzled by that. "He's the boss . . . maybe he made a commitment to them to help guard the shipments from Hangtown to the boat."

"He's the boss, but maybe not for long," Boulders said. "I think I'll mosey on up to the goldfields after next payday. I done saved enough for a fair stake. I could eat a bull on the hoof and spit out the hair, horns, and hide, but I've stomached Hutchinson about as long as a body can stand."

Clint extended his hand and Boulders took it in his ham-sized one. "I hope you hit the mother lode."

"Don't forget, we got a matter of bungholes and elbows to settle up one of these days."

"How 'bout February thirtieth," Clint said while Boulders ground his hand.

"That suits me jus' fine."

Boulders guffawed, slapped Clint on the back hard enough to put the average man on his face, then ambled down the gangplank and reboarded the Concord, waving as it pulled away. Clint watched him with some regret while the driver whipped up the team and the stage pulled away down

Front Street. Boulders had been a good man to have at his side, and one of the few who backed bluster with both brains and brawn. Clint hadn't believed the brains part at first, but Boulders had never gotten out of line on board the *Belle,* and he'd had many opportunities. No, Clint decided, he had plenty of mind to go along with the muscle.

Clint leaned on the rail watching the stage depart, and noticed an angry crowd forming on the dock, their voices raised in protest. Hutchinson had shut off ticket sales. Clint eyed the crowd a minute, then went to the deck gang boss and told him to hoist the gangplank. That, and placing a roustabout at each of the dock lines with a club, seemed to solve the problem. Disappointed, and grousing, the crowd dispersed to look for other ways out of the city.

Clint headed back to Stubby's office. The little man sat behind his desk, bent over paperwork.

"You got her locked up tight?"

"Tighter'n a tick'n hound's hair," Stubby said, looking up. "Adam's has the receipt for four bags with a total weight of five hundred and ninety one, pounds eleven ounces, lad. By far the biggest shipment yet.

"Do me a special favor with this one, Stub?"

"Anything I kin do, I will, lad."

Stubby hadn't even looked up when Clint had entered and Clint knew the little purser put far too much faith in the big safe. "Keep your office door barred and locked until we reach San Francisco. I'm the only guard aboard today, and this boat is crowded with riffraff who saw those Adam's sacks come aboard. I've just got a bad hunch."

"The little people givin' you the jitters, are they?" Stubby laughed. "You'll be havin' me miss me dinner."

Clint knew that by "little people" Stubby meant the leprechauns not the riffraff, as Stubby was a great believer in fairies and gremlins and ghosts. Everything good or bad that happened on the *Belle,* he attributed to them. He even wore a Druid charm around his neck for protection. To honor his newfound citizenship as an American and not tempt fate, he also carried a rabbit's foot in his trousers pocket.

"I'll go up to the kitchen and bring you down whatever you want. Just keep locked up today and don't open up for anyone."

"I promise, lad. No one but you and

Hutchinson will get in here until we hit San Francisco."

"You're a prince."

Clint fetched some cold chicken and a jar of lemonade for Stubby, then spent as much time on the main deck as he could, keeping Stubby's office in sight. Still he had to patrol the whole boat, as the main-deck passengers continually tried to get up to the salon where free food was available for the salon and private stateroom fares. The boat shoved off with a party atmosphere. Men broke out instruments and jugs, singing and dancing on the main deck in several competitive groups. Most could not care less that only a deck above, others traveled in relative splendor.

All of them seemed just glad to be alive, glad to be in California—even if she did shake and rumble once in a while.

They were safe on the beautiful *Benicia Belle*. At least they hoped they were safe.

10

Clint busied himself for the first hour of the journey by moving around the boat and watching. He wanted to keep close tabs on Farley Tucker, whom he knew to be trouble, and made sure he located him on each pass around the boat.

Covering the main deck from aft to stern, Clint worked his way through the crowd, then climbed the forward stairway to the hurricane deck, made his way through the private cabin passageway or around the *Belle*'s outside walkways, into the salon, across the boiler deck, then down the aft stairway to begin again. He left the pilothouse on the third level to Slocumb, who would resent his presence anyway. Besides, there was never anyone there but crew or an occasional invited guest.

Clint had made a half dozen of these forays when he decided to reverse the process.

As he started down the forward stairway he saw Garth Hutchinson on the forward deck, leaning over and looking down at something. He would have thought nothing of it, except he was again speaking with Farley Tucker. Clint started forward when Hutchinson arose and saw him coming. He said something to Tucker, who turned and headed astern around the opposite side of the boat. Garth seemed to be in a hurry.

"Something the matter forward?" Clint asked.

"Nothing. You take care of the master-at-arms job. I'll run the boat," Hutchinson snapped.

Clint shrugged and started back the way he had come.

"Slocumb wants to see you in the pilot-house," Hutchinson said, cutting his eyes around.

Clint glanced back over his shoulder. "What about?" he asked. It was unlike Slocumb to ask Clint to do anything.

"How the hell should I know? Just get up there. He is the pilot of this boat, Ryan."

Clint studied Hutchinson for a moment, wondering what was different about the man, then realized he had on rough canvas trousers, a linsey-woolsey shirt, and riding

225

boots—and the butt of a Navy Colt's showed its outline under the shirt. It was the first time Clint had ever seen him in casual dress and openly armed.

"You headin' up into the goldfields?" Clint asked.

"Are you heading up to the pilothouse?" Hutchinson snapped in reply.

Clint turned and started back up the stairway without answering, but the heat rose in his neck. God, he wished he could just go ahead and kick the hell out of Garth Hutchinson—but he needed his testimony. But in a few more hours he would no longer have to put up with Garth Hutchinson's moods. With that thought, Clint took the stairs two at a time.

"You don't have to run," Hutchinson shouted up after him. "Take your time."

Clint stopped and looked back at the *Belle*'s owner. The man was spooky as a hen under a hawk's shadow, and just as flighty.

Obligingly, Clint walked the rest of the way.

The pilothouse was reached via a ladder from the stateroom passageway, and it didn't take Clint long to reach it and start up. He mounted the walkway to the salon roof and banged on the glass pane in the pilothouse door. Slocumb looked over his shoulder. His irritation apparent, he waved Clint in.

Clint entered, but Slocumb kept his eyes glued to the river, not acknowledging his presence.

The Church of the River Redeemer appeared on the starboard side of the boat, and Clint walked across the pilothouse to watch it go by, wondering if Moses and his disciples had taken their own advice and fled the territory.

Apparently they felt they were above the wrath of the Lord, for they were busily working away.

Finally, Slocumb, whose red beard was growing back admirably, glanced over his shoulder. "You up here just to sight-see, or do you want something?"

"I understood you wanted to see me?"

"I don't need no help running this boat, Ryan. What the hell would I want with the likes of ya'll?"

Clint took a deep breath before he spoke. "You know, Slocumb, I don't mind a man not thanking me for saving his ugly hide from the river. I don't even mind a man not being cordial, so long as he's not offensive

. . . but you're one man who's about to get cross-grained with me."

"You mind your tongue, Ryan. I'll get you fired faster than buzzards jump a bloated goat."

"If you didn't have to run this boat, Big Henry, I'd whip your ass right now and shuck you over for the catfish to suck dry."

Henry Slocumb whipped his head around and glared at Clint, who took a step forward to assure Slocumb that he meant exactly what he said.

"As it is," Clint continued, when he was convinced Slocumb was not ready to pursue the matter, "I've already quit this job as of the San Francisco wharf. I'm through obliging anybody on board the *Belle*. Why don't you just amble off on the dock when we get there and I'll teach you some manners."

Henry Slocumb locked eyes with Clint, and for a second neither man moved, then both their heads whipped to port as a shot echoed over the din of the crowd and the churning of the massive side wheels.

Clint bolted for the door.

"Up here when you should have been below!" Slocumb yelled after him as Clint took the ladder two rungs at a time. Clint ignored him, jumped the last half of the ladder, and lit in the stateroom passageway. He jerked his Colt's as he ran for the salon. Charging in, he quickly surveyed the scene. Men still leaned casually on the bar, and the gambling games went on. A few men crowded at the portside windows, and Clint sprinted over.

"Where did that shot come from?" he yelled. Before they could answer, another shot rang out from below. Clint ran for the aft stairway and took the stairs three at a time, Colt's in hand. He reached the main deck, only to hit a wall of humanity—and to be pushed back up a few steps by a mass of running men. He fought against the tide and finally reached the deck.

Stubby! It's got to be someone after the safe.

Clint rounded the engine room and sprinted forward to the purser's office and crew's quarters. He checked behind him, still not positive where the shots had originated from, in time to see the crew aft pouring out of the boiler room and, to Clint's shock, diving over the rail and into the river. Two more shots rang out forward, then the boat's whistle gave a long solid keening wail—and didn't stop.

Clint moved forward. The door to

Stubby's office lay open. Clint eased to a walk, then flattened himself against the bulkhead, inching ahead, expecting the shooter to still be inside.

He took a deep breath, ready to plunge in, when he noticed a trickle of blood tracked the deck from inside the room. Clint leaped to the door and panned the room with the Colt's.

The safe door stood open, empty! Stubby lay on the floor on his face, his back a mass of blood and gore where a chest shot had exited. He had also been shot in the back of the head, and his face was partially blown away.

Anger overcame Clint's revulsion, and he started out the door to find whoever had done this, when he noticed that Stubby's arm was extended, and he had tried to write something in his own blood.

A bloody C marked the deck. Who the hell had a name beginning with C? No one he could think of, except himself.

Clint charged out of the purser's office in time to see one of the *Belle*'s two long-boats, which bracketed the pilothouse, drop past the outside of the rail from its tie down on the top deck. Henry Slocumb and two deckhands madly worked the block and tackles, lowering the boat much too fast.

"What's happening?" Clint shouted to Slocumb as he dropped past.

"She's gonna blow!" Clint heard, then the longboat hit the water and as quickly her blocks were cast off. Men milled in confused bewilderment all around the deck, but when they saw the pilot abandoning ship, cries arose in unison, and a dozen leaped over the rails and clung to the sides of Slocumb's boat. Others began dropping and diving from the salon deck above.

The whistle still keened its death song.

Slocumb and one of the other deckhands stood, picked up oars, and began viciously beating at the men clinging to her sides, who began to upset the boat with their weight and struggles to board her. They succeeded in knocking two away, but were still too close to the *Belle,* and another half-dozen men flung themselves over the side. Three of the longest jumpers landed in the boat, almost upsetting her completely. They knocked Slocumb down and the deckhand overboard. Others in the water reached her side and, with their added weight, finally pulled her gunnels under. She flooded, disappeared, and all the men were suddenly afloat.

Clint considered diving overboard himself, but hoped he had a few moments. Stubby's killer was probably forward, where the last shots came from. Besides, forward was as far from the engine room and boilers as he could get.

He grabbed two cork life rings that hung near the purser's office door and flung them into the water, then doggedly ran forward. Toward the killer, away from the boilers.

He covered the deck with the Colt's muzzle, then saw two men lying prostrate behind some firelight—trying to hide. Instinctively, he ducked, then saw they weren't moving. He edged all the way out onto the most forward part of the bow where they were, and stared down at the dead colorless eyes of Farley Tucker, his chest torn apart. The other man, whom Clint had seen with him earlier, lay nearby. Both dead from gunshot wounds.

A six-shot Allen's Pepperbox lay near Farley's outstretched arm, and the other Sydney Duck had an Aston cap and ball still stuffed into his belt. Clint picked up the Allen's. It had not been fired.

He scanned the river. They were just

passing the wide opening to Honker Bay, but he saw nothing. He looked aft. In the far distance, a half mile behind, a small boat bobbed along.

Then hell arrived in a roar, followed by scalding heat.

Clint found himself in the water, shaking his head, trying to clear his vision and stop his ears from ringing. He bobbed on the surface and saw the *Belle,* broken in half, her stern billowing fire and steam and smoke, disappearing under the roiling river. Men were in the water everywhere—some swimming for their lives, floating unconscious or bobbing along, waiting with death's patience for the river to suck them under. Her bow still floated, but Clint wondered how. He realized it was bearing down on him, either under the power of the current or driven forward from the force of the explosion.

He rolled onto his stomach and stroked as he never had before. Trying to outdistance a riverboat was ridiculous, he realized, and he rolled over in the water in time to see her bow begin to point to the sky as the shattered stern, or what was left of it, filled with water.

He wiped the water from his eyes and his

hand came away covered with blood. He felt his scalp and found a gash—stitch bad, but no worse, he decided.

Then he saw Rachel DuBois among the men jumping and being flung over the side from the wrenching of the dying boat. She clung to the rail of the *Belle,* hanging on desperately, her flowered dress billowing in the wind. When the bow pointed up at a sharp angle, unable to hold on, she dropped away, twenty feet to the surface, just before the *Belle'*s bow section shuddered a last time and disappeared under the water— sucking Rachel DuBois down with it.

Clint began stroking against the current, trying to find the woman. He avoided two drowning men who would have clawed him under, then grabbed onto a piece of flotsam. A broad plank, over two feet across and a half-dozen feet long served him well. Positioning it in front of him, he kicked against the current. Men cried out all around him screaming for help or crying in pain. Other flotsam, planks and pieces of deck and bulkheads and freight and furniture, some smoking and aflame, bobbed by. Smoke and steam lay over the river, blocking his view and hindering his effort to find the woman.

Clint had seen it all before, and the first time was still vivid in his mind. Suddenly a billowing piece of flowered cloth floated nearby. A portion of it had trapped some air, and Clint realized it was Rachel's dress. He lunged for it, but soon realized that Rachel did not fill it. He kept kicking against the current and watching. Abruptly, directly in front of him, Rachel DuBois cut through the water. She, too, avoided the men who thrashed all around. *Hell,* Clint thought, *she swims better than I do.*

Clint yelled and got her attention, and she stroked over with the current and joined him, grabbing onto the plank. She was clad only in her cotton chemise, and Clint caught himself admiring a little yellow fabric rose sewed to the chemise in the cleft of her bulging breasts and trying to keep his eyes from the dark circles under the wet fabric as she rolled to her back and paddled easily alongside him.

"You all right?" Clint asked.

"Hell no, I'm not all right," Rachel sputtered, her coal-black hair plastered across her brow, but her eyes flashing beautifully as always. "And you're bleeding like a poked pig, she said with concern.

"It's superficial. Let's kick together and get to shore," Clint said, offering her a position at his end of the plank.

"I don't need that thing, now that I got rid of that damned silk dress." She pushed away from the plank. "I damn near drowned trying to get that bloody gown off. The only time in my life I couldn't find a stinking man more than willing to help me unbutton—and there were men all around me . . . if you can call 'em that." Rachel began swimming toward the shore, a hundred yards away. Clint saw a man struggling to stay afloat, kicked the plank over closer then shoved it to him, carefully keeping out of his grasp. The man, scorched and singed, gave him a grateful look and grabbed the board.

Clint followed Rachel, swimming along behind her.

They dragged themselves out of the water among some river willows to find other men had reached the bank. They flopped down, not saying anything, breathing deeply, glad to be alive.

Finally Rachel caught her breath. "That rotten no-good son of a bitch," she spat out. No more had she uttered her epithet than she tore away a piece of her petticoat, wadded it, and applied it to the gash in Clint's scalp. He winced, but she persisted.

"Who?" Clint finally asked, still a little out of breath himself.

"Who what?" she asked, studying the cut.

"Who's a son of a bitch?"

"Garth Hutchinson, that's who."

"Have you seen him?"

"I saw him . . . rowing away from the bow in a longboat, just before the whistle went crazy and hell broke loose. The bastard knew she was going down. What a rat."

Clint stared at her, somewhat amazed at her language, trying to weigh this new information. "You saw him leaving from the bow?"

"He was even with my stateroom porthole when I looked out and saw him, all alone, merrily rowing away."

"Did he have four green sacks in the boat with him?"

"How the hell should I know? The whistle started going crazy about then, and I knew something was wrong—otherwise why would Garth be off in a longboat?"

"Good reasoning," Clint said, a wry smile crossing his face. He understood now what had happened.

Odds were, Garth Hutchinson had gotten away with the Adam's Express shipment of gold and was about to make a $250,000 insurance claim.

None of which Clint particularly gave a damn about, except for two things: he'd killed Stubby O'Flarraty in the process; and Clint, as master-at-arms, had been responsible for that shipment. Not to speak of a couple of hundred other dead and maimed men. Clint rose and studied the scene around him.

They had survived the earthquake threat only to be caught helpless in the devious plot of a common thief.

No, Clint thought. He would give Garth Hutchinson one thing—he was a very uncommon thief.

But he would not get away with it.

Clint pulled off his shirt and gave it to Rachel, then went about helping men out of the water and doing what he could to tend the wounded. Finally Rachel, too, arose and followed him about. Her chemise was drying and not so revealing as it had been, and Clint's shirt covered some of what her chemise had left exposed. Clint was pleased to see that she fell right into the nursing.

As Clint worked he replayed the last few

minutes aboard the boat in his mind. The two shots he heard must have been, first, the chest shot that put Stubby down, then the head shot when the robber—presumably Hutchinson—realized Stubby was still able to write and was doing so in his own blood. It hadn't been a *C* Stubby was writing, but the beginning of a *G*. The second two shots were the ones that killed Farley Tucker and the other man. Hutchinson obviously did not want his accomplices to be able to testify. What Tucker and Hutchinson were looking at over the bow rail and under the overhanging deck had been the longboat the getaway boat.

Then Hutchinson had sent Clint on a wild-goose chase up to the pilothouse. Hutchinson had made sure Clint was the only guard on board. Slocumb had not wanted him at all—Hutchinson had merely wanted him as far away from the purser's office as he could get him, and the pilot house was just that.

One question remained unanswered, but Clint knew where to solve it. Johann Probst, the boat's engineer, lay nearby on the beach. He had taken in a lot of water, but had been recovering well the last time Clint had seen him.

Clint made his way back through the river willows to where Probst reclined.

"Johann. What the hell happened to cause her to blow?"

"I vas given the order to pour der vood to her." He paused to cough. "More vood, more vood." The man shook his head in consternation. "Then the pressure suddenly vent too high . . . much too high." He coughed again, trying to clear water-filled lungs. "The safety valves . . . the blowout emergency valves—dey was stuck and did not work. We knew she vas gonna blow, and called to Herr Slocumb to blow 'is whistle. To warn ever'one. I tried to warn ever'one."

"Why was Slocumb calling for more wood? Didn't you have enough of a head of steam up to reach Benicia?"

"It vasn't Herr Slocumb on the voice pipe. Herr Hutchinson stuck his head in several times. He said vee vanted to race another boat up ahead . . . you know how the boys love a race. Dey jumped to."

"And the emergency blow-off?"

"Someone drove spikes between the hinges and the pipes. She couldn't vork. I tried to knock 'em out," he said, looking a little guilty. "Dey just vouldn't go, an' it

240

was too late . . . too late. Who vould do such a t'ing?"

Clint thought the man was going to break down and cry.

"I'm sure you did all you could. You were set up. Hell, we all were."

They worked until darkness fell, when boats began arriving to help in the rescue effort. There was little anyone could do. Rachel had found Joshua, and Clint, Rachel, and the black boarded a scow and headed back upriver to Sacramento with a number of other survivors.

Clint tried to engage Joshua in conversation, but the man gave him his back and walked away, to Clint's bewilderment.

Clint walked over to where Rachel lay among a cradle of coiled hemp rope and lowered himself down beside her as she sat up. "What's Joshua's problem?" he asked her.

"Problem? He's got no problem that I know of, other than being half boiled by that damn steam and tossed into the water like a toad."

Clint laughed. Maybe he had misread Joshua, expecting him to engage in a conversation after what he had just been through.

He couldn't help but press Rachel on the subject first and foremost in his mind. "Well, Miss Rachel, what do you think of Mr. Garth Hutchinson now?"

Her eyes reflected a mist, then she swallowed and looked away. "Disappointed, I guess." She hesitated a long minute, then stared out into the darkness as she continued. "He asked me to make sure you got good and drunk last night. Even asked me to get you into my room if that was the only way to keep you drinking—that's the first time he ever asked me to do something like that. I wondered why; now I know he wanted you sick, not able to do your job today. My attempt at a drunken assignation failed miserably." She finally looked at him, and her eyes smoldered. 'That much I regret.

"He didn't need me drunk," Clint said, ignoring her innuendo. "I failed bad enough cold sober and feeling just fine." He angrily thought of Stubby's torn body on the purser's office floor.

"No one man could have covered that whole boat, Clint. Don't blame yourself for what happened." She laid her head on his shoulder.

Clint's voice lowered. "Stubby O'Flar-

242

raty was my friend, and Garth Hutchinson shot him down like a dog. If I had been—"

"You can live your life with if's . . . I have. *No one* could have covered that boat, and Garth Hutchinson made damn sure it was packed to the hilt today."

"How did Garth do that?" Clint asked, confused. "Moses McClanahan predicted the earthquake, and that was why—"

Rachel's head came off his shoulder and she shook her head as she explained. "Garth Hutchinson *paid* Moses to shovel that bull to the *Sacramento Placer.* He told me it was a way to drum up business, and I fell for it. He was damn sure right about the business part."

Clint sighed deeply. Somehow, knowing how well planned the robbery and sinking had been gave him little solace. Rachel laid her head back on his shoulder as he leaned against the scow's rail and thought. He started to ask her where she thought Garth Hutchinson might have gone, but realized by her deep breathing she was asleep. It would have to wait, he decided, and then he, too, dozed.

When they arrived at the Sacramento City embarcadero, Rachel, wrapped in a blanket, followed by the faithful Joshua

243

made her way into town to find a room. Joshua had said nothing to Clint during the trip upriver, and Clint put it off to the strain of the wreck, but when he tried to shake hands with the man on leaving the scow, Joshua turned away again. Something was wrong.

Rachel was too exhausted to worry about it. In fact, she hardly noticed as Joshua followed her into town. Clint didn't understand it, but was still too damn tired to worry about much of anything. He accepted an offer from the scow's captain and slept on the small workboat.

The next morning, after borrowing an undershirt—the only thing available—from one of the scow's hands, Clint went straight to the first paper hawker he saw and got a copy of the morning *Sacramento Placer*. The headline read, BEAUTIFUL BELLE ON BOTTOM! The article went on to describe the wreck in great detail. No mention of the missing Adam's Express shipment was made, nor was any cause attributed to the affair.

Clint went in search of Rachel and stopped in three hotels before he found her registered at the Golden Nugget.

"What room?" Clint asked the clerk.

"We don't give out that information on lady guests," the clerk replied, looking at Clint—torn and dirty, blood still caked in his hair, clad in a sleeveless undershirt like he had just crawled up out of the swamp.

"Then you go rap on her door and tell her Clint Ryan's in the lobby."

That at least got a glance of acknowledgment from the man. "She left this for you," he said, and fished Clint's shirt from under the desk. Holding it between thumb and forefinger as if it had the pox, looking down his nose, the clerk handed the soiled and bloodied garment to him. "We don't wake our guests, man or woman," the clerk said, going back to his paperwork.

Clint put the filthy shirt on over the undershirt since wearing only the latter was considered rude.

"Then find her man, Joshua, for me. Is he out back in the livery?"

"A man came for him earlier, said he was taking him to San Francisco to rejoin his owner."

"Hutchinson?"

"His owner. That's all I know."

"Damn," Clint said. But at least he knew where Garth Hutchinson was.

The clerk eyed him up and down again.

"If you're going to await Miss DuBois, please do so outside."

Clint had serious thoughts about reaching over the desk and shoving the clerk's quill pen down his throat, but instead, he took the man's advice and went outside.

He rounded the building and went to the livery's water trough and washed up. He was drip-drying when two men Clint had never seen before rounded the corner of the hotel, also heading for the livery. He glanced behind him, and two more exited the barn door, heading his way. He thought nothing of it until one of the first two stopped in front of him.

"Clint Ryan?" he asked, a friendly enough smile on his face.

"Who wants to know'?" Clint asked, suddenly wary.

"You *are* Clint Ryan?" the man asked again.

Clint realized he still had the *Belle*'s master-at-arms badge pinned to his shirt. "Yes, not that it's any of your business—"

One of the men behind him slammed the butt of his rifle across Clint's head, and he went down like a box of rocks.

He had no idea how long he had been out, but his head felt like someone was banging away with a sledgehammer from the inside. He got a sense of being shipboard, and a feeling of relief flooded over him. Shipboard wasn't bad. He took three deep breaths. Musty, like deep in the bowels of a wooden vessel. He opened his eyes.

"Som'bitch!" he yelled as he stared into a set of yellow eyes. The rat went one way and Clint the other. He scooted across the wooden floor, sat up in the semidarkness, and backed into something solid. He felt behind him a network of flat iron, riveted together. "Damn the flies," he muttered, and his spirits sank. Using the bars, he pulled himself unsteadily to his feet. He bent and brushed himself off, and the floor moved.

He'd been in a jail before, so that was no great shock to him. Why he was here was another question, and a jail with a floor that moved, rocked? The *La Grange!* He had to be on board the *La Grange.* His eyes began to clear and he focused on his surroundings.

He was in one of a row of cells deep in the hold of the old ship. Other men watched him in silence, lying on their bunks or leaning in mute conspiracy against the flat-iron bars of their identical five-by-eight cells.

The rat worked its way back into the cubicle. Clint glowered at the animal, then tried to kick it, but missed badly.

"Don't be kickin' ol' Roddy," a voice came through the bars.

Clint moved to the opposite wall of the cell, a pace and a half, and fixed his eyes on the dark frame of a skinny man leaning there. "Pet of yours, is he?"

"They don't allow no dogs or parrots in here, pilgrim. It's Roddy the rodent and a couple of cockroaches, or nuttin'—but the roaches is big as yer thumb."

"How long have I been here?"

"Only a couple of hours."

"Anybody mention what the hell I'm doing here?"

"Don't ya'll know?" he said, his voice ringing with sarcasm. "Must be somethin' bad, 'cause you're down in the dungeon with the best of us. Nothin' but killers here on the bottom."

"Pardon me? I didn't kill anybody."

"Sure you didn't, pilgrim." The skinny man laughed hollowly, and moved away from the bars to his narrow bunk.

Clint, too, lay down on the hemp-rope-laced bunk and tried to think even though his head pounded. He was still there over an hour later when a shaft of light shot down the hallway between the cells and he heard a door slam. He rose and moved to the bars and heard footsteps. A guard, a mass of keys jingling in his hand, walked past.

"Hey!" Clint called, but the man didn't stop.

"Hay's for horses, boy," he said, and cackled nastily, but didn't slow.

"What the hell am I in here for?"

The guard hesitated, then walked back to Clint's cell and stood glaring through the bars. "I had friends aboard the *Belle,* you lousy bastard. You couldn't rob and sink her when she was damn near empty. You had ta wait till she was full a' folks. I'm a-gonna enjoy watching you swing an' I hope they leave you swingin' till the crows pick yer eyes." The man spun on his heel and started out.

"When do I get a hearing?"

"If I had my way, you'd get heared only while you was yelling for forgiveness, right afore they dropped ya'll through the trap-door."

"That's not an answer."

"True," the man said, "but you don't deserve no answer." He passed through a door at the other end of the hallway.

Clint returned to the bunk and waited. Night came and went, and they brought him a piece of bread and a bowl of watery soup for breakfast, laughing when he asked for coffee. It was hours later when they finally came for him. He began to believe he was in real trouble when he saw four guards gather outside his cell, then open it only after he was spread-eagled and leaning against the back wall. Two held rifles on him, while the other two affixed rub-raw iron shackles to his wrists and ankles.

"Where am I going?" Clint asked.

"To hell, I hope," one of the guards barked, then shook a short club at him. "Keep your mouth shut if you don't want to be gummin' pieces of yer teeth."

Clint decided to take his advice as they led him, shuffling and clanking, out of the cell.

11

His day went downhill from there.

He rode into Sacramento City in the back of an open wagon, in plain view of the people on the street, who gathered behind and followed the wagon to the small two-story courthouse. By the time the guards jerked him down into the street, over a hundred of Sacramento City's citizens stood decrying him and threatening to hang him right there. The guards hurried him inside, but the crowd filled the small courtroom and didn't quiet until a man with a full gray beard splayed across his chest and gray eyes so intense they could bore holes in cast iron, rapped the gavel and took a seat. But silence reigned for only a second before the crowd again began calling for his hanging. Again the judge rapped the wooden hammer until he achieved quiet.

"You gentlemen speak up again and I'll

find you in contempt of court and you'll spend the night in jail. And you all know I mean it." He got the quiet he wanted.

"Bailiff, bring the charges."

A stout, officious-looking man rose from one of the two tables facing the judge —Clint and the guards sat at the other— and waddled up and handed the judge a piece of parchment. The judge adjusted brass-framed eyeglasses, unfolded and perused the paper for a moment, then looked up.

"First, I'd like to commend the city attorney for the promptness with which he prepared these charges after receiving the depositions from San Francisco. Now to the business at hand. Mr. John Clinton Ryan, you are accused of one hundred and—what is it, thirty-three now? Yes, one hundred thirty-three counts of murder, of grand theft, and"—the judge chuckled— "of blocking a public transportation route." He looked at Clint over the top of his glasses. "That last charge is a misdemeanor, and I appreciate the city attorney's ardor, but I wouldn't be surprised if you aren't around long enough to serve the one year it carries. How do you plead?"

"Don't I get an attorney?" Clint asked

quietly, and the crowd shouted again until the judge banged them silent.

"You do, if you can afford one. If not, then we'll see if we can get a volunteer. Or you can represent yourself."

"Mr. Clifford Stanhope in San Francisco represents me."

This news raised the judge's eyebrows. The man sighed deeply, seemingly having trouble accepting that this might not be a cut-and-dried matter. "It'll take time for Stanhope to get up here. You sure I can't just ask one of the local boys—"

"Stanhope represents me. Who has charged me?'

The judge tapped his fingers nervously on the desktop. This was a turn of events he had not anticipated. Stanhope would certainly complicate matters. The crowd began to stir again, and he had to bang them quiet. "The city attorney brought the charges; he also serves as the county attorney, who also serves as the prosecutor." He waved the paper at a man in city coat and cravat who sat at the other table. "Mr. Alfred Bolton, there."

"On what grounds?"

"Mr. Bolton, do you want to answer the accused?"

Bolton cleared his throat and began to ruffle through a sheaf of papers in front of him. He looked up as if there were so many grounds he would not bother to read any. "I have quite a number of statements here obtained in both San Francisco and from the survivors here in Sacramento, the most damaging of which is a charge made by the *Belle's* owner—former owner I guess I should say—Mr. Garth Hutchinson, an eyewitness to John Clinton Ryan's killing of the purser, Mr. Sean O'Flarraty, and a witness to the robbery. His man Joshua has also made a statement, testifying that he saw where the dying man wrote the defendant's name on the deck in his own blood. A dying declaration condemning this man, this heinous murderer."

"Bull!" Clint roared. "I saw what Stubby wrote."

The judge banged the gavel again. "You'll get your chance in court," he said, and turned back to Bolton, who continued to read a half-dozen statements, none of which was as condemning as Hutchinson's. Clint searched the courtroom wondering where in the hell Rachel DuBois was, or Henry Slocumb, or Johann Probst, or anyone who could help him. But the crowd was a sea of angry faces. All looked as if they wanted blood.

And he thought there was a good chance they were going to get it as a mob of screaming wild-eyed men crowded around the wagon on the trip back to the *La Grange,* and the guards seemed less than enthusiastic about holding them back. Clint was hit with a number of stones and splattered with mud from the road as the wagon moved through the streets, but their jeers hurt him even more.

He was almost glad to be back in his dim musty cell.

That afternoon, a copy of the *Sacramento Placer* circulated through the bottom deck of the *La Grange.* The headline read CULPRIT CAPTURED, MURDERED 133. Clint's gut turned over when he strained in the dim light to read the worst news among many horrible allegations in the page-long four-column article. Pilot Henry Slocumb was listed among the missing. Slocumb, who could testify that Clint was in the pilot-house when the shooting began.

No one came to see him the rest of that day. He had to get the hell off the *La Grange* and clear himself. It was his only chance. He spent hours studying the cell and looking for a way, any way, to escape. By the time darkness fell, he felt discouraged and frustrated. The *La Grange* was heavily built and the cells well constructed. It looked like the only way out for Clint Ryan was going to be via a knot with thirteen turns.

Where the hell was Rachel DuBois? Where the hell was Don Carlos Vega? Where the hell was *anyone* who could help him?

He slept badly.

Someone shook him awake. The cell was pitch-dark except for a lantern the man held, wrapped so only a sliver of light leaked.

"You 'bout ready to git on down the road?" a deep rumbling whisper asked.

Clint shook his head, trying to clear the cobwebs, knowing he knew that voice— then it came to him and he bolted up. "Boulders! What the devil—"

"Keep it quiet. We only got one guard on our side, an' he took a little convincin'. We don't wanna get those other half dozen interested in what's a-goin' on here. An' one of these here other boys might yell out, figurin' on getting a little better treatment."

"We?"

"Toy and me decided you was bein' buried under a pile of hog slop." His eyes narrowed in the thin light of the lantern. "You didn't sink the bloody *Belle,* did ya?"

"No!" Clint snapped much too loudly. "And I damn sure want to get the bastard who did."

"Hell, I was kinda hopin' it *was* you." Boulders chuckled quietly. "Figured you might share if 'n we sprung ya."

Even in the dim light, Boulders could read the disappointment on Clint's face. "Don't go gettin' yer back up. It don't matter," he said, slapping Clint on the back. "We're a gonna spring ya anyways."

As they talked in a low whisper Boulders led him out of the cell, and Toy pushed a man inside, his hands bound behind him. Toy gagged him, tied his feet, and none too gently lowered him to the floor. Then he turned and followed as Boulders led the way down the dark passage.

"They's a-patrollin' the deck. We don't wanna be seen," Boulders said, but Clint had surmised that by the way he was pussyfooting around.

Boulders climbed a ladder to a thick plank door, pushed it open a few inches, then moved out onto the deck.

Clint followed, taking a few deep refreshing breaths, realizing again how musty and dismal the hold was. Lanterns cast an eerie light into the fog surrounding the *La Grange*. Boulders quickly made his way to the riverside rail and had to feel along it to find what he sought. As soon as he made contact with the line tied there, he slipped over and out of sight. Clint followed, staring down into the darkness, then hearing the reassuring sound of Boulders alighting in a boat. He, too, slid down the line. Toy followed, and in moments the boat had silently drifted a hundred yards downstream, where Toy and Clint manned oars as Boulders took up the tiller.

"Where'd you get the boat?" Clint asked.

"Some kind soul left her tied at the embarcadero."

"Where're we going?"

"Hell, away from the *La Grange*."

"Suits me," Clint said, smiling for the first time in days.

By an hour after the sun rose—at their backs now a the river had made its slow turn to the west—they were nearing the entry to Honker Bay. They had passed a number of scows and flat-bottomed mackinaws during the journey, but the men aboard paid little attention to them. Clint motioned to Boulders, who pushed the tiller hard over and they grounded on a mud bank. Clint made his way afoot to the wood yard and carefully studied it before walking in where a half-dozen men were beginning work. Within minutes he was aboard a *carreta*, cracking a whip over a pair of oxen on his way to the hacienda of Rancho del Rio Ancho—with Toy and Boulders fast asleep in the rear of the rickety cart.

Clint went straight to the establo when he arrived, and found Don Carlos and Sancho working in the tack room. Both the don and his head vaquero looked up as Clint entered. Neither spoke or offered a hand.

"I need three horses," Clint said, ignoring their slight. "And a gun." Boulders and Toy were both armed, but had not thought to bring an extra weapon for Clint.

"Under the circumstances," the don said, his voice hard, "I see I will have to rely on the *abogado* Stanhope to go to Monterey."

"That might take days and we don't have time. I'm going to take those affidavits to Monterey and I'm going to talk to Beale myself."

"I thought you were in jail."

259

"I was. I escaped."

"Then you are still wanted for murder," the don said coldly.

"Your partner is responsible for the *Belle*," Clint snapped. The don's expression slowly melted from hard to confused. Clint continued, "Garth Hutchinson sank the *Belle*."

"That is ridiculous—" the don began.

"Ridiculous unless you're running a boat losing thousands of dollars a week, unless you're trying to cover the theft of several hundred pounds of gold, unless you're trying to cover a murder you've committed—three in fact—and last but certainly not least, unless you stand to collect a quarter of a million dollars in insurance.

The old don's face began to harden again. "Still, *you* are the one wanted for murder and theft."

Clint pondered for a moment, then he looked up. "Send Sancho with me. He can go on to Monterey with my letter to Beale explaining that I couldn't bring them myself, and with the affidavits, if they catch me before I can clear my name."

The don glanced at Sancho. "Three good horses, and you will go also." Sancho grabbed his reata from a peg on the wall along with four lead ropes, and disappeared out the door to the remuda. Don Carlos crossed the barn, reached behind a plank in the wall, and removed a small bundle, then returned to where Clint waited, unwrapping it as he walked. He handed Clint a .31-caliber five-barreled Allen's Pepperbox, a brass powder horn, a ball bag, and a box of caps.

"This is a gun I keep in the barn for emergencies."

"Thank you, Don Carlos," Clint said with sincerity.

Don Carlos centered his eyes on Clint. "I hoped . . . I knew in my heart that these rumors were not true.

"He did a good job of setting me up, Don Carlos, but I'm not sunk yet. There were witnesses, and I'll find them, and I'll bring Garth Hutchinson to the judge in Sacramento if I have to drag him bouncing behind a horse all the way."

Sancho reentered the barn, leading four strong horses, and they quickly saddled and bridled them.

With meat-filled tortillas in hand, the four men rode out of the hacienda yard. Clint glanced over his shoulder and saw

261

Apolonia standing near the open front door. They locked eyes for a long moment, but neither waved nor acknowledged the other. Clint turned back to his mission— a task that would determine if he had any future in California—and led the way, gigging the tall gray he rode into a lope. In fact, he thought as they picked up the pace, a mission that might determine if he had any future at all.

Every lawman in California must have already been looking for him, or would be soon, not to speak of every man who knew or was related to one of the many victims on board the *Benicia Belle*. The more he thought about it, the more he understood Don Carlos's concerns. It would be a wonder if he was not shot down in the street long before he was able to get to Stanhope, or certainly before he could catch up with Garth Hutchinson.

Boulders went into Benicia and made arrangements for a boat. Clint and the others waited in a sandpaper-oak grove on a slope overlooking the river until the flat-bottomed mackinaw made its way downstream and nuzzled into the shore, then they rode down and loaded the horses.

While they worked, the *River Ruler*

passed. News of Clint's escape would reach San Francisco long before he did.

They reached San Francisco shortly after dark—too late to try to reach Stanhope and pick up the affidavits—so Clint, backed up by the other three, rode straight to the offices of the San Francisco-Benicia-Sacramento Steam Navigation Company on Long Wharf. A crudely worded sign plank was nailed across the door, OUT OF BUSINESS.

With a knot of fear in his gut, worried that Garth Hutchinson might already be on a steamboat back to New York, Clint reined the gray around and headed into the city. There were two dozen hotels and boardinghouses in San Francisco, and Clint set out to check them all. Each time he saw a man wearing a city marshal's badge, he was forced to go the other way. He considered going to the livery and picking up Diablo and his things, but reconsidered, wondering if they might be watching his horse, hoping he would do just that. He could go after the big palomino only when he was ready to ride out to Monterey.

They decided to try the big hotels first and had already checked two when Clint walked into the three-story New Englander and strolled nonchalantly toward the desk. But before he reached it, he stopped short and turned away. Joshua stood waiting nearby. The lobby was filled with men many of them unsavory looking characters who Clint decided were Sydney Ducks.

Until then, he had thought the New Englander to be one of the classiest hotel in the city, and was surprised by the low-class characters who filled its lobby. Joshua was talking to a pair of the men. Clint stepped behind a post and watched until a waiter exited an adjoining room, carrying a tray with a bottle and glasses. He handed it to Joshua, who turned and headed for the stairs.

Clint followed but held back, staying a floor below as the man climbed all the way to the third, then climbing the last flight only high enough so that he could see over the top riser and down the hall, where Joshua rapped quietly on a door. Clint could not see who answered, but they only accepted the tray then the big black turned and started back down the hall. Three at a time, Clint returned to the main floor and hurried outside to where the others waited by the horses.

"I think we've found him. Either Hutchinson or maybe Rachel DuBois." Either one would do for a start, Clint thought as he surveyed the building. He noticed that the building next door was only two stories tall, and the distance from its roof's edge to the wall of the New Englander was no more than six feet. He had considered simply rapping on the hotel-room door, but he didn't know who was in the room—Garth Hutchinson, Rachel, or someone else. And he sure as hell couldn't trust Joshua, if the last time he had tried to have a conversation with the man was any example. If Rachel was with someone else, or alone, he didn't want her to know he was here and looking for Hutchinson—he was sure she would warn him if she thought she might get something out of it. But maybe, just maybe, if he could get on the roof of the building across from the window, he could see who was there, and then he would know what to do.

He turned to Sancho, Boulders, and Toy. "I've got to get on that roof," he said.

"Simple, amigo," Sancho said, mounting the roan he rode. "Come on."

He reined over to an alley on the far side of the two-story building and disappeared down it. Clint and the others mounted and followed. By the time they turned into the dark lane, Sancho stood atop his saddle at the rear of the building and was shaking out a huge loop in his reata. The two-story was flat-roofed, and near where Sancho had stopped, a two-by-two-foot brick chimney rose four feet above the top story. Sancho easily looped the leather rope over the chimney, but did not draw the wide loop up tight, and motioned for Clint to move his horse under the line and climb up it. By stepping into the foothold created where the loop came back to the reata, he was able to reach the edge of the roof and quickly pull himself up and over.

He crossed the roof and searched until he found the lighted window of the room where Joshua had taken the whiskey, crossed his legs, and sat down to watch until someone came into his field of vision— only a few inches between the curtains. It was only a second before he got much more than he had bargained for. Rachel stepped in front of the narrow opening and removed her gown.

Clint took a deep breath as she continued. Guiltily, he glanced over his shoulder, but he had to watch in order to find out who, if anyone, she was with. He was even more embarrassed by the fact that he was beginning to enjoy it as Rachel continued to undress, until she stood beautifully buck-naked.

Clint could not see who they belonged to, but a pair of well-muscled arms encircled her and pulled her away from the window. *If that's Garth Hutchinson,* Clint thought, *she must not have been too disappointed in him.* In a second the light dimmed.

Clint recrossed the roof to climb back down, but luckily he looked first. A man, afoot, stood shaking his finger at the mounted Sancho, Toy, and Boulders. Clint ducked back as Sancho looked up, then the reata slid off the chimney stack. Clint could hear the horses clomp out of the alley and peered over again to see as the man walked back to the street where two others waited. Catching the gleam of light off a shield on one man's chest, Clint again moved out of sight and returned to his spot by the window.

He stayed there a long while. Finally, a scraping sound jerked him alert, and he realized as a shadow moved away from the window that someone had opened it. He considered hanging from the roof and dropping to the alley below, but he would probably turn or break an ankle, and that was the last thing he needed right now.

What he needed was Garth Hutchinson.

The two-and-half-foot-high-by-three-foot opening beckoned him, as he figured he could make the six-foot jump easily. He walked to the street side of the building and looked down from its waist-high parapet. Boulders, Toy, and Sancho stood leaning against a hitching rail, not looking up.

"Hey!" Clint called softly.

Still not looking up, Boulders spoke loudly. "They're still watching us."

"I'm going in."

"How the hell . . ." Boulders started to ask, but Clint was already moving back across the roof.

He aligned himself with the window. The room was totally dark now. He hoped they were asleep after their little rendezvous. Then he charged across the roof and launched himself at the open window.

He slammed into the sill, half in, half out of the opening, then lurched through.

"'Who's there?" He heard a shrill cry, then bedsprings creaked and footsteps pattered toward the hall door. Clint plunged forward and slammed into the running person, dragging whoever it was to the floor with him. He caught the small wrists and pinned them.

"Who are you?" Rachel's voice cried out.

"Is Hutchinson here?" he asked, easing his hold a little on her wrists.

"No! Clint? I thought you were in jail."

Beneath him, Rachel lay all but naked in a thin nightgown. He struggled to his feet and helped her up. She moved to a bedside table, flamed a sulfur head, and lit the lamp.

"Where's Hutchinson?" Clint pressed, trying to keep his eyes from the clinging nightgown.

"Hutchinson doesn't sleep with me," Rachel said indignantly.

"Maybe not all night. But he was here," Clint challenged.

She cut her eyes away. "You saw."

"Enough."

"He's staying at a cheap hotel. He doesn't want the investigators from Adam's Express or from the insurance company to think he has any money left."

Someone rapped on the door, and Clint pulled the pepperbox from his belt.

Rachel crossed tentatively to the door and leaned close. "Yes."

"I heard noises, Miss DuBois. Randell, from the desk. Are you all right?"

"Yes, thank you."

"There are three men at the desk asking about you."

"That's probably my men," Clint whispered, guessing that Boulders, Toy, and Sancho had seen him make his leap and were trying to find out what room she was staying in.

"Tell them to wait."

The man's footsteps disappeared down the hall.

"What hotel?" Clint asked.

"Are you going to kill him?" Rachel's eyes were filled with concern.

"Not unless he makes me. I want him to confess."

"He'll never do that, Clint."

"Then you'll testify for me."

"Me? What do I know? I heard some shots and the whistle, then the ship exploded."

"You know he paid Moses McClanahan to lie about that earthquake story."

"So what does that prove, Clint?" She shook her head. "You need someone to testify that you weren't there when Stubby was killed, and you need to find that gold."

"Where is the gold?"

"He wouldn't tell me, you know that. Hutchinson trusts nobody."

"Not even the woman he beds?" Clint immediately regretted these words.

"No. Not even me," she said, the hurt apparent in her voice. "I think he must have hidden it in the delta. Somewhere in those miles and miles of streams and tules. No one will ever find it if Hutchinson doesn't want them to."

"Then I've got to follow him there."

"No one can testify that they were with you when Stubby was killed?"

"Henry Slocumb . . . but he went down with the *Belle*."

Rachel studied him for a long moment. "Garth Hutchinson is my meal ticket, Clint. That's all he is to me. I don't approve of what he did, but I don't want to lose my livelihood, and I don't want to go back to singing and being ogled by thousands of grubby men." She crossed to the window and stared out for a moment, then turned back. "I like you, Clint. I've always had a certain feeling for you, and I don't want to see you take the blame for what Garth did. Still, he's a dangerous man, and he, would probably kill me if he thought I went against him.'

271

"What are you driving at, Rachel?"

"Big Henry Slocumb is alive."

"Where?" Clint asked excitedly.

"Down on the Barbary Coast somewhere. Garth just left here with a half-dozen Sydney Ducks he'd hired to act as bodyguards for him and to help him find Slocumb. He means to kill him. Slocumb told someone that you couldn't be responsible for Stubby's killing. And word got back to Garth."

That explained the Sydney Ducks in the lobby when Clint first got there. "Where exactly is he?"

"He's hiding out, drunk and embarrassed about losing another boat. I don't know where exactly."

"Then I've got to find him before Hutchinson," Clint said, bolting for the door.

"Clint! Joshua is with him. Don't harm Joshua. And Clint . . ."

He hesitated.

"Be careful."

He smiled and winked at her, then turned serious. "You don't need Hutchinson, Rachel . . . or anybody else." He turned and hurried out, but heard her voice behind him.

"Sometimes we just take the easy way."

He ran out the door, down the three flights of stairs and through the lobby, where his *compadres* waited.

"Damn," Boulders said, joining him on the way to the door and shaking his head. "I thought you was a-thinkin' you was a bobwhite, the way ya'll sailed across and into that window."

"There was a beautiful half-naked woman waiting," Clint said.

"Well, that makes a little more sense," Boulders said with a guffaw. "I might coulda flied like a hawk my own se'f," but then his smile faded as they opened the door and came face-to-face with the three city marshals who had run them out of the alley.

They didn't move or step aside.

A barrel-chested man stepped into the light flowing out of the hotel door. A reflection gleamed off the shield on his chest as he eyed Clint up and down. The other two stood side by side, close behind him.

"You hold up a minute, partner," the thick-chested man instructed, putting a stubby hand on Clint's chest. He pulled a piece of paper from his shirt pocket and unfolded it. "We're a-lookin' for three men. A John Chinaman, big as an ox." He cut

273

his eyes to Toy. "A gnawed-eared lout, ugly as a dog's butt." He eyed Boulders up and down. "An' a fair-haired light-eyed fella name of John Clinton Ryan." He reached over and flipped Clint's hat off.

The other two deputies took a step back and went for the guns at their hips. In a leap, Boulders was on them, slamming their heads together. They went down in a heap.

The barrel-chested man clawed for the Navy Colt's at his side, but Clint smashed a right square on the man's chin. His eyes rolled up in his head and he went over backward like a felled oak—but not before Clint grabbed the Colt's out of his hand. He shoved it in his belt as they ran for the horses. Clint took two steps then slid to a stop and returned for the paper. He looked and ran at the same time. A wanted poster with a thousand-dollar reward showed a drawing of him and had written descriptions of Toy and Boulders. It hadn't taken Adam's Express long, he thought.

"Don't let me forget who that deputy was," Clint yelled at Boulders as they mounted. "I'll need to return this Colt's as soon as we're through with Hutchinson."

"Hell with him," Boulders said indignantly. "Hell with any som'bitch thinks I'm dog-butt ugly."

"You're pretty as fifty double eagles to some folks," Clint shouted, handing Boulders the wanted poster as they spurred the horses. Boulders stared at it, then wadded it up and threw it in the road.

They pounded down the planked city street and, horses sliding, made a turn onto another until they were out of sight of the pile of deputies. They reined up to a steady walk, and Clint explained to them where they were going and what they were up against.

Now all of San Francisco would know he was in the city. He didn't have much time.

12

They rode down out of the lit streets of the city to the dark waterfront. Clint thought about splitting up so the saloons could be checked faster, but even two men traveling alone along the Barbary Coast were subject to the shanghai gangs and brigades of thieves. So they stayed together. Sancho held the horses while Clint, backed by Toy and Bloulders, charged through the saloons. Searching. Searching for his alibi, Slocumb, a man others searched for. Searching for his future in California.

Searching for the man who had killed his friend in cold blood.

But eluding his pursuers at the same time. Even San Francisco's city marshals traveled in groups of five or more along the Barbary Coast, so they weren't hard to spot, and Clint was able to avoid them easily.

It was near midnight when he entered Orval's Ale 'n' Chops. He searched carefully, kicking through sawdust and peanut shells on the floor of the clapboard building, eyeing each of several dozen men in the dim smoked-filled light. Henry Slocumb should have been an easy man to spot, always given as he was to frock coats, brocaded waistcoats, and high hats—and, of course, that red beard.

Boulders and Toy reclined on the bar while Clint moved among the men.

But when Clint finally did spot him, he was clad in the rough clothes of a denizen of the Barbary Coast with a floppy-brimmed hat pulled low over his eyes. His beard had been shaved but had regrown in a rough stubble, and he stared oyster-eyed into a half-finished mug of ale in a dark corner. Clint looked over his shoulder for Garth Hutchinson or any of the Sydney Ducks he might recognize from the lobby of the New Englander. Satisfied that he had beaten the competition, he shouldered his way through the rough-looking customers and pulled up a stool across from Slocumb.

Eyes watery, Slocumb looked up from his beer and slowly focused on Clint.

"Hello, Henry."

"Ryan. How's it feel to be out of a job?" he said, slurring his words slightly.

"There's another one down the road."

"Not for me," Henry said. He shook his head sadly. "Not for me."

"The *Belle*'s sinking can't be blamed on you."

"Ever'thing that happens to a boat is blamed on the pilot," Henry mumbled, then drained half the beer he had left.

"Not by me, Henry. It wasn't your fault, and I'll shout that from the highest hill."

Henry looked up with appreciation. "That's kind of ya'll. But it'll do no good."

"Still, I'd do it. Would you do the same for me?"

"Wha'da'ya mean?"

"You haven't heard that I'm wanted for killing Stubby?"

"All I've heard is the barman settin' down another beer."

"Well, they think I did it, and that I robbed the *Belle* and that I was responsible for the sinking and the death of all those other men."

"Hell's bells," Henry said as a slow drunken smile crept across his red-blotched face. "You was with me when the first shots rang out. 'Sides, I never figured you for smart enough to pull off a robbery like that. Leon, the barman, said ya'll was in the salon when the others was heard."

That wasn't exactly right, but Clint was not going to quibble. Actually, he had been on the main deck when the last shots rang out—but Stubby was already dead. "Then I'm innocent, right?"

"As a newborn babe," Henry muttered.

"I've got some bad news for you, Henry," Clint said in a level voice.

Henry looked up, then began to laugh. "Hell, bad news dogs my trail." Then he seemed to get interested. "What bad news?"

"Garth Hutchinson robbed the *Belle,* caused the sinking, and wants . . . you . . . dead."

Henry stared, uncomprehending. Clint went on to explain that Hutchinson had blamed the sinking and the robbery on him, and that Garth had heard that Henry was Clint's only alibi.

"You'd better stick close to me and my friends, Henry, until I can get your statement to a marshal. Once you've done that, there'll be no reason for Hutchinson to do anything but run."

"Hell . . . I'm happy right here."

279

"Will you be happy to be dead as a mackerel, right here?"

That seemed to sober him. "When can I make this statement?"

"In the morning, as soon as I can get you to my attorney."

"I thought ya'll said I had to talk to the marshal."

"You can, after you make a statement to my attorney. I can't exactly waltz right into the marshal's office at the moment."

"Let's have one more beer, then we'll go?"

"Let's go. I'll get you another beer wherever we find you a room." Clint rose and scanned the room. "Come on, Henry."

Just as Henry tried to rise, Clint pushed him back down. Garth Hutchinson had shoved through the batwing doors and stood studying the room. Joshua, even bigger than the well-muscled Hutchinson, stood at his rear.

Clint eyed Toy and Boulders, who leaned on the bar sipping a beer. They had not seen the big former owner of the *Belle*. Clint rejoined Henry and sat.

"Don't get up, Henry," Clint advised. "Hutchinson just walked in."

Henry began to quake like Moses had predicted California would.

"Calm down, Henry. I've got help, Toy and Boulders, at the bar." Clint didn't mention that Hutchinson probably had at least a half-dozen tough Sydney Ducks with him. As the thought occurred Hutchinson's entourage followed him into the saloon.

Just when Hutchinson spotted Toy and Boulders at the bar, Henry Slocumb suddenly rose, knocking his stool aside, and bolted for the rear door. All hell broke loose in Orval's Ale 'n' Chops.

Hutchinson yelled at his Ducks, who charged forward after Henry. Toy extended a massive arm and clotheslined two of the Ducks as they ran by. Boulders went after Hutchinson, but Joshua stepped in front of him, and Boulders was stopped by three other Ducks before he could reach either of them.

Clint wanted to go after Henry, but he had to help Toy and Boulders. He charged across the saloon, knocking men and tables aside as he did.

Hutchinson, backing for the door, clawed for his gun while Toy and Boulders dispatched the Ducks in quick order. Just as he reached the batwings Sancho crashed through, knocking him aside—but he recovered and ran out, followed by Joshua.

"The marshals come. At least a dozen," Sancho yelled. Most of the Ducks lay sprawled on the floor, and the two left on their feet were more than willing to retreat as the big men headed for the door to join Sancho and get the hell out of there.

"I'm going out the back!" Clint yelled, racing out after Henry Slocumb.

He ran under a sign—PRIVY—over the door leading out the back, made a short hallway in a few steps, then ran into the darkness, his Allen's in hand—and stumbled over something on the ground between the rear door and the little privy building a few steps beyond. He knelt to find a man, prostrate on the ground. Clint's heart clawed up into his throat. It was Henry. Slocumb lay with his throat sliced from ear to ear, and blood was puddling the hard ground around him. Already, his heart had stopped pumping.

"Damn, damn, damn," Clint swore. Then he heard the sound of footfalls in the hallway behind and ran onto a side street.

"Here!" Boulders's voice rang out, and Clint ran to where his three mounted *compadres* waited with the horses. Clint swung into the saddle just as shots rang out behind him, and bullets cut the air around him with their hum of death.

The men gave heels to the horses and galloped up the street out of sight.

Finally they slowed to a walk.

Clint's mouth tasted sour and his stomach rolled. He had had Henry safe in hand and lost him. Henry had been a pompous ass at times, but he didn't deserve to die. Hutchinson had won again. Now the only way Clint could prove himself innocent was to find and return the gold.

And the gold was probably in the middle of two hundred square miles of delta mud, tules, and swamp.

An impossible job, unless Garth Hutchinson led him to it.

Clint, with Boulders at his back and Toy and Sancho watching the roof next door, checked Rachel's room—this time rapping on the door. He was sure Hutchinson wasn't there, as none of the Sydney Ducks were hanging around the lobby. After a moment her voice rang through. "Who is it?"

"It's me."

The door opened a crack, then swung wide. When Rachel saw Clint wasn't alone, she reddened and stepped quickly behind the door to hide the fact that she was clad only in the thin nightgown. "It's late," she said, peeking around.

"He didn't come back here?"

"No. I told you, he's got a room at some cheap hotel."

"Which one?"

A little disgruntled, she repeated, "I told you, Clint. I don't know."

"He killed Slocumb." At this news Rachel paled. "Slit his throat, or at least had someone do it."

"If I knew where he was, I'd tell you, Clint."

They left. Clint paused only long enough to borrow a quill, ink, and paper from the desk clerk and quickly pen a letter to Edward Beale in Monterey. It was obvious, as Don Carlos had feared, that he would not be able to go there personally.

There were twenty-five cheap hotels and boardinghouses in the city, and checking them all at this time of night would be impossible. So they rode a ways out of town and slept on the ground in a scrub-oak grove. Clint slept badly. He was risking the freedom—or worse—of Boulders, Toy, and Sancho. If he were back on the Kaweah, it might be years before anyone figured out where he had gone. Maybe the best thing for him to do was run, he thought, then cursed himself for it. No, he had no choice. He had to prove himself innocent.

Shortly after dawn, they were back in the city, waiting outside Clifford Stanhope's office.

Stanhope arrived early and quickly ushered Clint inside. "They've been watching my office," he said conspiratorially. "Word came that you wanted me to defend you."

Clint had worried that the stuffy attorney would have nothing to do with him, so he was pleased at his greeting.

They entered Stanhope's private office. The attorney removed his coat and hung it on a coat tree, then sat behind the large maple desk before he spoke. "How much gold did you get, Ryan? I heard almost six hundred pounds."

The look of disappointment must have been clear on Clint's face.

"Are you going to tell me you *didn't* rob that boat?" Stanhope asked, and the look on his face became more disappointed than Clint's.

"No, I didn't rob that boat. Garth Hutchinson did."

"Robbed and scuttled his own boat . . ."

Stanhope pondered a moment, then chuckled softly. "Got the gold shipment, and I suppose the *Belle* was well insured."

"A quarter of a million," Clint offered.

"Well, good for Hutchinson. She was a losing proposition, as will be any boat that tries to go against the California Steam Navigation Company." He settled back in his chair. "I was looking forward to a nice fat fee to defend you."

"There were over a hundred men killed when he sank the *Belle*," Clint said, glaring at the man, amazed at his attitude. But he wasn't here to judge the lawyer's morals. "I need those affidavits on the Vega matter."

"Fine," Stanhope said, but made no effort to move. "You owe us another hundred and seventy dollars."

"Just get the affidavits and send a bill to Don Carlos. He'll get your money here."

"No deal. You pay me off, and then you get the statements."

Clint took a couple of steps and leaned his knuckles on the broad maple desk, glowering down at Stanhope. "Don't you realize I'm wanted for killing one hundred and thirty-three men, Stanhope? One more won't make a tinker's damn. In fact, you son of a bitch, I might just enjoy it."

286

Stanhope flushed. Until now the man had always been remarkably cool. He rose quickly, crossed the room to a closet, and opened the door. Two four-drawer file cabinets stood inside. He opened a drawer and removed a sheaf of papers and, having regained his composure, handed them angrily to Clint.

"One hundred and seventy dollars, Ryan. And if I don't collect it from Don Carlos, I'm holding you responsible." Clint moved to the door as Stanhope rattled on. "And I don't want a bunch of damned chickens or goats—"

Clint slammed the door while Stanhope was still talking. He couldn't help but smile as he descended the stairs, remembering a story he'd been told the night before while searching the bars for Henry. Over two dozen lawyers already practiced in San Francisco. A bartender had asked him, "What do you have when you have a half-dozen lawyers at the bottom of San Francisco Bay?" When Clint shook his head, the man had informed him, "A good start!" It had been the only light moment in a bad night.

Within minutes after Clint had left the building, Sancho was on his way, affidavits

287

and letter to Beale wrapped in his bedroll, and Clint was just as happy to have him gone. Sancho had been a good friend for many years, and Clint did not want him mixed up in his problems. Now Sancho would be out of it.

Now, what the hell to do.

He picked up a copy of the *San Francisco Call* while they hunted for an inconspicuous place to eat breakfast. Clint didn't open the paper until they were seated in a tent on the edge of town. On a stove out back, a big Norwegian flipped flapjacks high in the air. For a half-dollar each, provided by Boulders, they sat to all the pancakes and syrup they could stuff down and all the coffee they could drink. Only when they had finished did Clint open the paper. He read the headlines, then a small article in the lower corner of the front page caught his eye: SCARSDALE, RODERICK, & ST. CLAIR REFUSE BELLE CLAIM. He went on to read that they had not really refused the claim, but had refused to file the claim until after an official hearing, to be conducted by the harbor commission, which would ascertain the cause of the accident, or the sabotage, whichever it was determined to be. Even then it might take many months, for the lion's share of the money would have to come from Lloyd's of London. But the *Belle* was insured even for acts of sabotage, so long as it was committed by parties other than the insured—Garth Hutchinson.

Clint's name was mentioned, but only as a suspect in the matter. It was the first ray of light he'd had, and he suddenly realized that San Francisco might not have the ardor for his conviction that Sacramento had. Then he remembered the thousand-dollar reward. Hell, everybody in California would want to see him caught, if they could collect. Guilty or not. Conviction or not.

Then another thought came to him. If the insurance wasn't going to pay off right away, maybe Garth Hutchinson would run short of money and have to go back to his stash of gold.

But waiting was not in the cards. Every hour Clint spent in San Francisco brought him closer to a rope. Finally, dejected, he talked the problem over with Boulders and Toy.

Toy, normally good for about five words a day, spoke up. "Prophet Moses boat in harbor. You go there and wait. He owe you. Tong will tell us when Hutchinson leave. Tong knows all things."

"Moses." Clint thought about it for a moment. "I don't know that he owes me—"

"He owe you. Not for him, few men be on *Belle*. His saying earthquake come cause many men to die. You being blamed. He owe you."

Moses had to be feeling real bad about now, Clint thought, agreeing with Toy's analysis. And if they followed Garth Hutchinson back to the delta, they would have to have a boat. It wasn't a bad idea, and it would keep them out of sight. In fact, it was a damn good idea. The city marshals wouldn't be wandering around a boat—particularly a church boat named *The Lord's Work*.

"Let's go find Moses," Clint said, and they left the café tent and mounted up.

By noon, Toy was leading the horses away to a livery, and Clint and Boulders were aboard *The Lord's Work*, face-to-face with an irate disciple of the Prophet Moses, who was on an errand.

"You can't wait on the boat!" the man shouted adamantly, shaking his finger at them and beginning to attract the attention of other people on Hodgkin's Wharf and on other boats nearby.

Boulders, in his pointed way, reached out

and grasped the man's pointing index finger and put him to his knees. The disciple paled, and Clint was afraid he was going to be sick right there on the deck.

"Let's us go below and talk this over," Boulders said. Using the finger to lift and guide him, he led him into the boat's small cabin. In an hour, Moses returned to the boat carrying a box. He flushed with a shocked look when Clint climbed out of the cabin.

"Lord have mercy,"Moses began. "You're a wanted man, Clint Ryan. I thought you'd be halfway to Texas by now."

"No reason to run since I'm not guilty."
"Well, I can't hide you aboard *The Lord's Work*—"

"Afraid you might ruin your reputation?" Clint asked sarcastically.

"Guilty or not, you're wanted by the law."

"I wonder how knowing that Garth Hutchinson paid you to spew that garbage about an earthquake would set with the law. Considering Garth Hutchinson robbed and sank the *Belle* . . . with a couple of hundred men on board who wouldn't have been there had it not been for your lousy prediction."

Moses turned white as a shroud.

"They might even think you were an accomplice."

Moses looked over his shoulder to make sure no one was paying any attention to the fact that he had a wanted man on board his boat. Then his gaze centered on Clint. "Let's go below an' talk on this."

Within minutes Moses had agreed to loan *The Lord's Work* to Clint and to find another way back to his church for himself and the disciple, who still had a pained look on his face. His only proviso was that Clint would say he had borrowed the boat without Moses's knowledge if he was found out.

That night Toy returned to the *Work*.

Rachel DuBois had sent word via Joshua, who sought out the tong, that she wanted to see Clint.

"It's a trap," Boulders warned. "That Joshua is Hutchinson's man."

"Hutchinson's slave, and owning a man sure as hell doesn't gain his respect or loyalty. She wouldn't set me up."

"She's a woman, ain't she? Crafty as a snake an' more slippery. Don't go."

"I'm going."

Boulders sighed deeply. "Why don't we

292

jus' take this here boat and sail off? The Sandwich Islands sound real good right about now."

"You getting soft on me, Boulders?" Clint asked as he strapped his belt back on and shoved the Colt's he'd "borrowed" from the deputy through one side and the little Allen's Pepperbox through the other.

"I'll bang heads with a hundred men, Clint Ryan . . . but I never had much use for women, less'n it was to warm my bed."

"I'm going."

"Hell, you're hardheaded as my ol' pa. Then I'm a-going, too."

"Have it your way."

Without being asked, Toy tagged along. Boulders, too, carried a Navy Colt's, and Toy had an old muzzle-loading pistol, but he also carried a tong hatchet that he must have purloined from their headquarters. This time they were afoot, as Toy had not brought the horses back from the livery where he had taken them. Clint decided it was just as well, since the marshal's deputies they had run into at the New Englander had seen that they were on horseback and the San Francisco marshals would be looking for mounted men—although they probably thought the three of them were long gone by now. Prudent men would have been.

It was a long climb up the hill to the New Englander, and they were all puffing by the time they approached. There was no sign of the Sydney Ducks outside the hotel or in the lobby. Clint asked Toy to wait outside the front door, with strict instructions to get the hell out if any marshals came near, and asked Boulders to follow him upstairs, but to stay a floor below.

Clint walked boldly to Rachel's door and rapped, the Colt's ready in his hand.

The door opened slowly. Rachel wore an apprehensive look on her face—and a black eye. Clint shoved his way in.

"I'd just as soon you didn't see me like this," Rachel said her voice about to break. Clint surveyed the room. When he was sure no one else was there, he reached out and took Rachel in his arms. Immediately, she began to cry softly, then, as he held her closer, to sob.

He waited quietly for her to finish, then held her at arm's length. "Hutchinson?"

"Yes. 'When he came back, Randell, the desk clerk, told him someone had been in my room. I guess he overheard us when he came to the door. Hutchinson was furious.

He thought I was seeing another man. . . . I had to tell him it was you."

"It doesn't matter," Clint said quietly.

"I told him you forced your way in here."

"I did. Jumping in the window is not exactly being invited."

"True. But I would have let you in if you'd come to the door."

"Did you find out where he's staying?"

"Yes. The New South Wales. It's on the Sydney Duck side of Telegraph Hill."

"I've seen the dump." Clint thought for a minute.

"I think he owns the place, although he's got it under somebody else's name. He's always sending people to stay or eat or gamble there. Everyone there is in his debt, at least."

"Hell, we might as well end this thing. I can't wait much longer, hoping he might lead me to the gold." Clint headed for the door.

"Clint," she said softly.

He turned back.

"He told me to tell you where he was if you came back." Clint nodded. "Be careful, he's got a bunch of men. Maybe as many as two dozen, maybe more. They've taken over the New South Wales."

"Thanks, Rachel," Clint said, but hurried on. Again her voice rang out as he moved down the hall.

"Please don't hurt Joshua."

Hurt Joshua? Clint thought, taking the stairs three at a time. The black was big as a stallion and hard as the hubs of hell. Keeping out of Joshua's way was more on his mind than trying to hurt him. He picked up Boulders on the second floor and hurried on down the stairs.

In the lobby, Clint hesitated then crossed to the desk, where Randell stood waiting on a pair of guests. Clint reached across the counter and snatched a turn in the man's cravat, dragging him up onto his own desktop. The customers scattered.

Clint glared at the man, nose to nose with him. "Rachel DuBois's business is her own. Do you understand?"

"Yes, sir," the man muttered, his eyes wide, his cheeks quivering.

"If I hear you've stuck your ugly nose in her affairs again, I'll stomp your gonads into a greasespot right here in your lobby."

The man paled and Clint dropped him. He scooted back off to the counter and backed with palms flat against the wall, his eyes showing white around the pupils as Clint left.

Outside, Clint quickly explained to Toy and Boulders where Hutchinson was—and that he wanted Clint to know. Obviously, he was well fortified in the New South Wales and had plenty of men.

Clint felt that things were destined to end this night, at least between him and Hutchinson, gold or no gold. He told the other two men to get their horses from the stable where Toy had taken them and where to meet him, borrowed some money from Boulders, and went to get Diablo and his things.

It was an eight-block walk. He studied the place carefully as he approached, but no one was in sight. Diablo was in his stall, but Clint's tack was locked up tight in the tack-and-feed room. Clint would either have to knock the lock off or wake the hostler.

Clint decided on the latter.

The man came down and opened the door, then took Clint's money in payment. He gave Clint a strange look or two, but never said a thing about what Clint knew must be true—the marshals *had* been watching. As soon as Clint rode out, the man hurried out of the livery and down the street. By the time he found a marshal, or reached the marshal's office ten blocks away, Clint would be long gone.

It felt good to be astride the big palomino again. Diablo pranced and single-footed, happy to be out of the confining stall and, Clint hoped, happy to have old Clint Ryan on his back again.

As promised, Boulders and Toy awaited him at the foot of Calle de Fundacion. The west side of Telegraph Hill sported hundreds of Chinese shacks, the east side half as many Italian shanties. There was a no-man's-land in between since the two groups didn't mix. Along the north foot of the hill, the Sydney Ducks took over down to the waterfront. The New South Wales huddled at the foot of Telegraph.

Rooms bracketed a long hall on the second floor, and the rear of the first. Clint knew the front half of the first was a saloon and gambling hall. And the front of the building, although the rear was dug into the hillside, rose over a half story over the street, with a latticework of beams and posts and a long stairway up from the boardwalk. Men without means regularly slept behind the latticework under the front of the building. The space was well-known as cheapskate's cave.

Lanterns lined the eaves of the building on the front and two sides. The rear was dark. It was the best-lit building on the block.

Clint had decided to come at the place from behind, from off the top of Telegraph.

He figured their chances would be much better coming out of the darkness and the few scrub oaks that still grew where the hillside was too steep for buildings.

They rode up and over the hill, stopping at a spot high on the slope overlooking the Barbary Coast. Just fifty yards below squatted the rear of the New South Wales. The slope down to the hotel was too steep for other buildings, and other than a few scrub oaks, it was clear. As usual, the gambling hall and the street in front of the hotel were alive with rowdy men.

"You boys got any ideas about how to get the weasel out of his burrow?" Clint asked.

"Not without a match," Boulders said.

"Hell." Clint laughed quietly. "San Francisco's burned down so many times, maybe another wouldn't matter."

"I should have brought some whale oil," Boulders complained.

"I thought you were kidding," Clint said. He would never be surprised at what Boulders might do. "We'd burn the whole damned town down. We can't do that."

"Start landslide," Toy said quietly.

"Or a flood," Boulders said. "Or an earthquake," he added with a loud guffaw.

"No," Toy corrected, in all seriousness. "Landslide." He pointed across the slope to a pile of rock, most of which had been moved from building sites on up the hill.

"You know, that *would* shake things up a bit," Clint said, studying the pile of rocks. "If we could just roll one of those big ones over here and get it started down, I'll bet the folks would pour out of there like they did out of Sacramento to ride the *Belle* to the bottom of the river."

"Looks like hard work to me," Boulders groused.

"So's everything worth doing," Clint said, and reined over to where Toy was already testing a few of the huge rocks to see which one might roll well. He finally settled on one thirty inches across and, without awaiting help, put his huge shoulders and back into it. Boulders dismounted and helped him, cursing with each push. Clint picked up a smaller one and carried it to the spot where they figured they had the clearest shot at the hotel.

Before long, they had the thirty-incher in place and a dozen smaller stones surrounding it.

"Now," Clint said, puffing. "Let's see if the weasel can be flushed out."

13

With all three of them heaving simultaneously, they soon had a half-dozen boulders bounding down the steep slope. Clint watched, fascinated, as the rocks gained momentum, picking up soil and logs, becoming a single careening mass by the time it neared the rear of the New South Wales.

What have we done? Clint thought, wincing when the agglomeration smashed into the rear wall of the hotel, collapsing the clapboard structure with a splintering rumble, then continuing on unimpeded.

With the support of the back wall gone, the second floor fell in on the first. Then the rocks crashed through the first floor, tearing out the underpinning, and with a thunder and billow of plaster dust, the whole building toppled at an angle, the east side still on its stilts but the west wiped away. *My God, I hope the cheapskates weren't bed-*

ded down yet, Clint thought, but had no time to worry about it. The three of them ran for the horses.

Clint led the pack over the edge. Diablo set his hindquarters, alternately sliding and plunging. In hair-raising seconds they reached the New South Wales. Men poured out of what was left of windows and doors and rents in the walls themselves. Someone took up the call "Earthquake," and it echoed over the dust-filled darkness.

Colt's in hand, Clint rode down the west side of the hotel and around the front, then back up the east side. Boulders stationed himself on the west side and Toy in front, all of them searching quickly this way and that as three dozen men charged out of the wrecked structure. Many of the lanterns lining the New South Wales at its second-floor level had smashed, and flames licked up the splintered walls.

Where was Hutchinson?

A pistol barked in the darkness of the rubble and spat flame. Clint flew backward out of the saddle as if he'd been jerked with a line. He gasped for breath, rolled. and scrambled for the cover of some twisted timber, where he fell prone. He heard his name shouted over and over again,

"Ryan! It's Ryan! Gather up! It's Ryan! Get him! It's Ryan!"

He recognized Hutchinson's voice. At least this destruction had not been for nothing.

He reached down and ran a hand over his side. A bullet had hit his thick leather belt, careened on, and carved a groove in his side. His hand came away wet with blood.

Other pistols barked behind him, from where he had left Toy.

Diablo trotted back away from the flickering flames, throwing his head and whinnying. Clint rose to a crouching position and jammed the Colt's back in his belt. He charged across the space between him and the big horse, caught the reins and then the horn, and swung into the saddle without the use of the stirrups. Bullets cut the air around him, muzzle flashes burst from the darkness of the rubble. He gave the big palomino his heels.

Riding low in the saddle at a dead gallop, he pounded around the front of the building in time to see three Ducks charging out of the rubble toward Toy, who had flipped his fired single-shot pistol around and grabbed it by the barrel to use as a bludgeon.

But the charging Ducks had more in store for them. Toy held the tong hatchet in his other hand, hidden behind the horse. Gleaming razor-sharp metal met the head of a charging man and split it like a ripe melon just as the Duck's weapon discharged, spitting fire. Toy was blown back in the saddle and the second Duck to reach him fired but missed. He turned tail as Toy regained his seat and the gleam of the upraised hatchet in his thick arm convinced the Duck it was a place he didn't want to be. In two bounds he was lost in the darkness.

Clint shot the third Duck just as he leveled the muzzle of his shotgun on Toy, not ten feet away. Both barrels discharged when Clint's slug tore through his back, but luckily only blew up a plume of dirt under Toy's horse. That set the animal bucking, but Toy managed to stay in the saddle.

Clint spurred the palomino over to Toy. "Are you hit?" he yelled.

"Can fight," the big man said.

Clint galloped into the darkness, shouting, "Get out of the light of the flames!" and Toy followed.

"Where's Boulders?" Clint asked.

"He ran in," Toy said, in ever-more-laboring gasps, then Clint saw the growing patch of blood on his shirt. He leaned over and tore the cloth away. A bullet had hit him just under the collarbone and passed cleanly through. Clint stuffed a piece of the cloth into the wound, both front and back, then grabbed Toy's pistol and bag and reloaded his weapon for him, since Toy's left arm was useless. He handed it hack.

"Can you stay here and watch? I'm going in after Boulders."

"I can fight."

"Just watch. I don't want Hutchinson getting away. Just follow him, Toy, if you see him. Don't try to take him."

Toy nodded faithfully.

Clint circled around and came at the rubble from the back. Flames from the completely destroyed west side caught quickly and already licked at the sky above.

Clint would have preferred sitting this one out, waiting until the rats were driven from the warren, but Boulders was in there.

He heard more shots from inside.

Looping the reins around the saddle horn, Clint slapped the palomino on the rump to send him clear of the scene then charged into a fissure in the rear of the debris.

He squinted into the darkness, first bending low, then crawling on his hands and knees. As he moved forward smoke began to block his vision, and he felt the heat clawing at his face. He tripped over the body of a man. Almost face-to-face with the body, he made sure it was not Hutchinson. It was Joshua, and he was bleeding from a long gash on the head, but alive.

Clint tried to lift the big man, but some furniture and a section of fallen wall had him pinned. The heat grew more intense as Clint tried to move the load. He couldn't get it to budge. He ran back outside to Diablo and got his reata. Taking a quick turn around the horn, he ran back inside and fixed the loop under Joshua's arms, then returned at a dead run and mounted the big horse.

With Diablo's powerful hindquarters straining, the load suddenly gave way. Joshua banged from pile of debris to wall and back, lurched out, bounced and bruised but alive.

Clint ran back and removed the reata, then dragged the unconscious man a few feet farther from the growing flames.

"Sorry about the cuts and bruises, ol' buddy," Clint said more to himself than

Joshua. The big black coughed a few times, but with eyes tightly shut. "Better than fried like a fritter anyway."

Clint ran back and hunted for another opening. He moved around to the east side, where a good portion of the wall still stood.

He picked up a loose board and smashed a window, one of the few remaining unbroken, and quickly cleaned the glass away so he could climb through. Before he could, he heard running footsteps inside and ducked just as shots rang out and splintered the jambs.

"Boulders!" he shouted, his back to the wall, the building to the east now clearly lighted by the growing inferno. "Boulders!"

Shots rang out from the front of the structure.

A dozen or more.

Clint ducked and ran. Bobbing and weaving down the east side, a good portion of his progress in deep shadow of the remaining rubble, he found a gap and charged inside again. The opening was filled with smoke and Clint could see flames across the rubble of what must have been the saloon and gambling hall. The floor was canted badly. Tables and chairs, fallen beams, and angled pieces of wall littered his way.

Where the hell is Boulders? Where the hell is Hutchinson?

But he moved forward, working his way through the wreckage, panning the Colt's as he did so. He stepped on something, and bent to see he'd stepped on the face of a dead man. A beam lay across his chest. The big Turkish mustache. A Sydney Duck. He hoped it was one of Hutchinson's men, and that his landslide had not caused the death of some innocent gambler.

A shadow flickered across him and instinctively Clint dived for the cover of a tilted wall. Shots roared and shattered the plaster near his head, and he rolled again, deeper into the shadows.

The heat was becoming intense. *No one can stay in here,* he thought.

He heard bells clanging. He backed away from the encroaching fire. Seeing no more moving shadows, coughing badly, he escaped back through the crack in the wall. With his back to what was left standing, he worked his way around to the front.

The Monumental Fire Brigade, bright green brass-trimmed wagon and brightly adorned team of four matching gray horses, worked hard in the street near the hotel. Men uncoiled hoses and others manned the

309

long pump handles on either side of the wagon. As they charged the flames Clint worked his way away from the building.

He went to where he had left Toy, but the big man was nowhere to be found. A crowd of spectators was forming, and Clint began to work through them hunting for Hutchinson, Boulders, or Toy while the flames totally consumed the New South Wales.

Clint turned to watch, hypnotized by the inferno as were the rest of the bystanders.

Another fire brigade and a dozen marshals arrived. The latter began pushing the crowd back. Clint moved away quickly, not wanting to be recognized. He went to the rear of the watching throng, as far from the marshals as he could get and still see the fire, to watch for Hutchinson. The building to the east, twenty feet or more from the doomed New South Wales, caught quickly, bursting into flame as if it had been soaked in whale oil. The fire fighters abandoned the first fire to work on the second, for twenty feet to its west was another freestanding building, then a row of common wall structures. The whole town could go up again if it continued to spread.

Transfixed, Clint watched what he had

wrought. It sickened him, for so far it had been for nothing.

Then he felt the press of a muzzle in his back, and the words of a man speaking low, close to his ear.

"Just back away, Ryan.

Hutchinson! Clint turned slowly to face the man, and two mustached Ducks with pistols in hand at his sides.

Garth Hutchinson smiled tightly in triumph—a snake with a cornered squirrel.

"You bastard," Clint spat.

"Just move away with us so I don't have to shoot you down right here. Get his weapons, Alec." One of the Sydney Ducks, a man as large as his boss, reached over and took the Colt's and the Allen's out of Clint's belt, and the sheathed knife he always carried. Alec's hand came away with blood on it from the wound in Clint's side.

He wiped it on his trousers. "Some bloke hit 'im," he said. "I hope it was me brother."

"He didn't get out," Hutchinson said. "I saw him, dead as a nail under a beam."

"I saw 'im, too, boss," Alec said, glaring at Clint. "An' I'm a gonna 'ave me a time payin' this bloody bloke back."

Clint ignored him, but eyed the man he hunted. "Go to hell, Hutchinson," he said

311

adamantly. "If you're going to shoot me, you might as well do it in front of all of these witnesses."

"You're a wanted man, Ryan. Those marshals would pin a medal on me if I shot you down right here."

"Then why wait?"

"I'd have been happy to hunt you down and shoot you like the dog you are, but since you've made it so easy, I want you to be tried, Ryan. The publicity is good for my insurance claim." He leaned forward and lowered his voice so the Ducks couldn't hear over the din of the fire and the crowd. "The marshals are going to find a small cache of that Adam's Express shipment when you confess where you've hidden it—"

"You know better than anybody where that gold's hidden."

"Still, when we have you all night, and you show up knotted and bruised, the marshals will be convinced that I beat the hiding place out of you. They'll find only a very small cache, but it will be proof enough that you were the culprit."

"If you plan to turn me in, go ahead and turn me over to those marshals," Clint challenged, with a motion of his head.

Hutchinson backed away and spoke loud enough so the Ducks could hear.

"I'm not interested in turning you in until I have a cadre of newspaper men in tow and can make the announcement that you've confessed to sinking the *Belle,* and to where you've hidden the gold, in front of these boys."

"You always did like to do things in a big way."

"Hell, man," Hutchinson said, eyeing the growing conflagration and smiling ironically, "you don't do bad yourself. Let's go!"

As soon as they got away from the crowd, the big Duck Hutchinson had called Alec tied Clint's hands behind him tight enough to cut off the blood. Clint kept searching the darkness, hoping against hope that Boulders and Toy had survived the fight.

He was led to an alley, where Hutchinson had a buggy tied. A fourth man waited in the driver's seat.

"Ya got 'im, boss," the man said, and grinned a toothless smile. "I knew ye would . . . but he sure as hell made a mess of the New South Wales." Just then the pile of flaming rubble in the background fell in on itself, and a great billow of sparks soared into the night sky.

"Get in the buggy," Hutchinson instructed.

"Up yours," Clint said. Alec jammed a set of ramrod-hard fingers into Clint's wounded side. The pain almost took him to his knees, and he guessed he was shot a little worse than he had first thought.

"Now, climb aboard," Hutchinson said with a smirk Clint knew all too well.

"Where are we going?" Clint asked as Alec shoved him up into the rear seat of the buggy.

"Just shut up and enjoy the ride," Hutchinson said.

"You don t seem too concerned about the New South Wales," Clint continued. "I suppose it's insured, too?"

"A prudent man carries insurance," Hutchinson said, his blue eyes reflecting the ironic humor. The Duck driving whipped up the team.

When they finally reined up, Clint saw they were at the rear entrance to the New Englander.

"Rachel won't like this," Clint said, hoping against hope that this was true.

"She won't have to put up with you and

the rest of us but for one night, Ryan," Hutchinson replied. "She'll understand, seeing as how you burned our accommodations to the ground."

Rachel's eyes flared when Hutchinson shoved him in the door, but she said nothing. Alec and the other Duck, a man they called Checkers, tied him to a chair while the third man dropped Clint's Colt's and Allen's and the sheathed knife on a chest of drawers, then dug a crooked cigar out of his pocket and lit up, leaning against the wall to watch the fun. Rachel sat on the edge of her bed, wringing her hands, trying to act unconcerned—and doing a good job until Hutchinson gave Alec a nod, and he smiled, then drove a hard right into Clint's gut.

"Where's Joshua?" Rachel asked, trying to ignore the beating Clint was receiving.

"Dead, I think," Hutchinson said, seemingly unconcerned. "In the fire. Ryan here probably shot him."

Rachel turned gray.

Clint had not said a word, hiding his pain, but then he spoke up.

"That's a lie," he gasped out. "I pulled Joshua out of the fire. He's all right—"

Then another punch slammed into his midsection and he clamped his jaw.

Short-armed, but thick and strong, Alec hunkered down into his work. Punching a nonmoving target was his forte. And the punches that slammed into Clint echoed like clubs on a side of beef.

"Stop it! Stop, stop, stop!" Rachel shouted, able to stand no more, and reached for Alec. Hutchinson shoved her back on the bed.

"You don't like seeing Ryan take a little punishment?" Hutchinson asked her with a snarling grin.

"I don't like seeing anyone beaten," she said, her own eye still ringed with purple. "Stop it."

"I'll stop it when he tells us where he's hidden the gold." Garth laughed loudly.

Rachel stood, red in the face. She grabbed Hutchinson by the hand and headed for the door. "Come on," she demanded, and he followed, but not until he nodded to Alec to continue.

Even outside the door, she could hear the hard punches bury in Clint's stomach and chest, and the crack as the two Ducks took turns hitting him in the face.

"Obviously, you don't want these men to

know that you robbed your own boat," Rachel challenged.

"Of course not, darling," Hutchinson said, actually admitting for the first time that he had stolen the money. "We have to make this look good, or I won't get the insurance money, and if that happens, it might be years before we can travel—really travel, like we talked about."

"Make them stop, now, or I'll tell them myself that it was you, not Clint Ryan, who took the shipment . . . and they'll want a share.

Garth stared at her for a long moment, the thuds of the punches ringing through the door. His eyes grew cold.

"Now, Garth!" she said. "I can't stand this."

Finally he shrugged and opened the door. "Enough," he said.

"Hell, Hutchinson, I was just getting started," Alec groused, rubbing his knuckles with his other hand.

Clint's head sagged, his chin on his chest, and he appeared to be unconscious. Blood trickled from his ears and nose and ran in spurts from a cut in his brow. His cheeks were puffy and one eye was almost closed.

Hutchinson turned back to her. "Okay?" She nodded.

He turned to the three Ducks. "You boys sleep in the lobby or out in the livery. He won't be giving us much trouble, but just in case I'd better stay up here with Miss DuBois."

Alec and the other two gave each other knowing looks, but headed out. "He didn't tell nothing, boss," Alec complained. "I can get him to talk with a little more time."

"Hell, he's out cold already. Don't worry, Alec," Hutchinson said, patting the man on the back as he walked out, "you'll get your revenge. Here's a double eagle." He reached in his pocket and pulled out a coin. "You boys have a few drinks. Seeing him swing will be revenge enough, won't it?"

"I'd rather kill the bloke wit' me bare 'ands."

"That doesn't serve my purpose, Alec. Downstairs."

Alec and the other three left, the promise of a few drinks on the boss even stronger than their hope for revenge.

Hutchinson turned back to Rachel and smiled warmly. "Shall we get some rest?"

She looked at him a little incredulously. "You want me to climb in that bed with you, with Clint Ryan right here in this chair?"

"He won't be waking up probably till morning. And hell, woman, I want to celebrate. You got any whiskey here?"

Rachel's expression turned to disgust. She crossed the room to a chest of drawers, then pulled the top one open and removed a bottle. She stood staring at it for a moment, then turned back, smiling, her attitude changed completely.

"Garth, honey, when we get the insurance money, where are you going to take me?"

"Why, anywhere in the world, darlin'. With that and the gold, we're halfway to becoming millionaires."

Rachel poured herself a half inch of the fiery liquid and Hutchinson a glassful. Then she crossed the room, sat on the edge of the bed, and patted the spot beside her. "Come tell me about New York again, Garth, honey. While we finish off this bottle."

They drank and talked and killed the rest of the bottle, but Rachel was careful to drink only a little. Finally Hutchinson became amorous and began to nibble on her neck. With great care, she arose and slowly undressed while Hutchinson threw off his boots and trousers, leaving his shirt on, and turned the lamp down low.

Feigning unconsciousness, Clint watched out of the narrow slit in the eye almost closed by the beating, carefully straining at the knots that bound his hands —but they held tight.

As Rachel climbed into bed with Hutchinson Clint ground his jaw, and wondered just how the hell he was going to get to the guns and knife on the chest of drawers.

"Let me give you a back rub, honey," Rachel said in the darkness.

In moments, Garth Hutchinson was snoring loudly. Then, even the snoring stopped. It seemed an eternity to Clint, who continued to strain at the bindings, until the bed squeaked, and he heard quiet footfalls, then the knife—his knife—slip from its sheath. Either Rachel DuBois was coming to cut him free or to jam the knife between his ribs for shooting Joshua, as Hutchinson had claimed he had.

But the knife went to work on the ropes binding his hands.

14

Clint felt the bounds on his hand slip away, then the needlelike tingling as the blood began to return. Rachel slipped back across the room and into the bed. Clint's feet were still tied to the chair, but he waited to get the feeling back in his hands, rubbing his wrists, before he untied them.

He'd just bent to do so when someone rapped on the door. Clint sat back up and put his hands behind the chair as if he were still tied. Again the door rattled with a steady knock. Rachel arose, quickly pulled on a wrap, and tried to get to the door before Hutchinson awoke, but the big man sat up in bed, fumbling with a match and the lamp.

"Don't answer it," he snapped at her as she groped with the silk robe. "I'll get it." He rose, pulled on his trousers, and tucked the shirt he had worn to bed inside them.

He reached for his small Root's Pocket Pistol resting on the bedside table.

"It's me . . . Joshua," a deep voice said.

Hutchinson didn't bother with his pistol, just crossed to the door. "Joshua?"

"It's me, Mr. Hutchinson."

Hutchinson pulled the door wide. "I see you did get out of that mess." His voice was cold and unconcerned. "What the hell's so important that you bother me here, boy."

"Jus' wanted to let you know I was all right, sir."

"Thank God," Rachel said, and Joshua shot her a quick grateful look, but said nothing until his eyes fell on Clint.

"I see you gots him, sir."

"Go out and sleep in the livery," Hutchinson said, not the least interested in having a conversation with his slave.

"Yes, sir," Joshua said, turning away.

Garth Hutchinson locked the door behind him and started to return to bed. Rachel dropped the wrap away and climbed back in. Hutchinson hesitated, turning to study Clint, who still sat in the chair, his chin on his chest.

"Come on back to bed, Garth, honey."

"Soon as I check his ropes," he said, and took a step in Clint's direction.

Clint suddenly lunged forward, hampered by the chair but driving his head deep into Hutchinson's stomach.

The big man doubled and stumbled backward. Rachel screamed.

Clint hopped forward, dragging the chair with him, but even hindered, he managed to land two hard punches to Hutchinson's head before he recovered, then knocked the man careening over the corner of the bed. He sprawled on the floor in the narrow space between bed and wall.

Clint made a quick choice between trying to fight the big man with his legs bound to the chair, or going after the guns. He choose the guns and began to hobble back across the room. He tangled in a hooked rug and fell.

Hutchinson was on him before he could rise, pummeling his head and ribs.

"Stop it!" Rachel demanded with authority.

Hutchinson rose and gave Clint a final kick in the ribs, then cut his gaze to Rachel.

She held the little Allen's Pepperbox leveled on Garth's stomach.

"What are you doing?" Hutchinson asked incredulously.

"Just move away from him and stop."

"Give me the gun." Hutchinson took a step for her, but stopped short as she ratcheted the hammer back.

"Rachel! Give me the gun."

"Just . . . leave. Just walk out of here."

He looked at her strangely, then looked over to Clint. "He'll get away if I leave . . . and we might lose the insurance money. Besides, Rachel"—he gave her a condescending look—"who will pay for this room if I leave you." Garth edged forward a half step.

"I don't care about the insurance money, or any of your money," Rachel said. "You leave now. I don't care if I ever see you again."

Clint reached down and fought to untie his ankles, sliding the chair with a rasping sound as he did so. Rachel glanced at him.

With another half step, quick as a serpent, Garth slapped the Allen's away then brought the flat of his other hand across Rachel's face with a vicious crack. She sprawled across the bed.

"Don't be doin' that, sir," Joshua's voice rumbled from the doorway.

"How did you get that door open?" Hutchinson snapped.

"Jus' don't be hittin' Miss Rachel."

A smirk slithered across Hutchinson's

324

face. The Allen's lay on the floor between him and the big black, with the Colt's atop the chest of drawers only two steps from both of them.

"I want him out of here," Rachel said to Joshua, but the expression on Joshua's face didn't change, nor did he look at her.

Without hurrying, Hutchinson walked over to gather up the Colt's. Before he could get his hand on it, Joshua stepped forward and clamped an iron grip on his wrist.

"Miss Rachel wants you to go."

There was a long moment of silence as Garth Hutchinson stared into the big black's eyes.

"You're my man, not hers, Joshua. Maybe you're forgetting that. I could sell you out of here on the next cattle boat, and her captain might just keep you in the pens."

"Yes sir," Joshua said, but he did not release his grip. "Still an' all, ya'll better leave."

"All right," Hutchinson said quietly, backing away from the chest of drawers. Joshua released his grip on Hutchinson's wrist, who stepped around him as if to depart.

Clint managed to free the knots on his ankles and toss the rope away.

When Hutchinson reached the doorway, Rachel mouthed a quiet "Thank you," and Joshua nodded.

Hutchinson shoved him violently, sprawling him across the bed on top of Rachel, then snatched the Colt's up off the chest of drawers. At the same instant Clint dived for the Root's on the bedside table and Joshua bounced back and leaped for Hutchinson. Rachel rolled off the bed onto the floor. The big black closed with Hutchinson before Clint reached the bedside table, and Hutchinson's Colt's roared, reverberating in the confined space.

Joshua wrenched Hutchinson's gun hand, his other hand on his throat. For a second Clint thought no one had been hit, then blood poured down Joshua's back. Clint swung the Root's just as Joshua sagged to his knees, his right arm hanging uselessly. Hutchinson recocked the pistol and pressed its muzzle against Joshua's forehead.

"Don't do it," Clint said coldly. He had his own pistol leveled on Hutchinson's chest.

Hutchinson glanced over and realized

for the first time that Clint had the gun. "He's my man, I'll kill him if I damn well please.

"Not without dying."

Rachel rose from the floor, Joshua's Allen's in her hand. She cocked it and took two steps. Slowly and deliberately she raised it and pressed the muzzle against Hutchinson's temple. "And I can guarantee what Clint says," she offered quietly.

Hutchinson smiled tightly. "Well, I guess we've got a standoff."

"Drop the gun, Hutchinson," Clint said.

"Fat chance.

"I don't give a damn about that man," Clint said convincingly. "I'm going to put a fine hole in your head . . . unless you drop that gun."

Clint could see a flicker of doubt darken Hutchinson's eyes.

Clint didn't weaken, but Rachel did. "No, Clint," Rachel pleaded, dropping her pistol to the floor. "He'll shoot Joshua. I know him.

Hutchinson locked gazes with Clint. "I'll do it, Hutchinson," Clint threatened.

Joshua, on his knees in front of Hutchinson, managed to recover the Allen's Rachel had dropped and swung it up to

Hutchinson's lower belly before the man realized what was happening. The Root's roared.

Hutchinson's Colt's spit flame at the same instant.

Joshua was flung back, rolling half under the bed. Hutchinson dropped the Colt's. His hands groping for his stomach, he stumbled back against the chest of drawers and collapsed to his knees. The room lay hazy with the gunpowder, and the stench filled their nostrils.

Clint kicked the Allen's and Hutchinson's Colt's away from his reach.

Rachel dropped to her knees beside Joshua. He was bleeding badly from a gaping hole in his neck, but said nothing.

"I'm shot. I'm shot," Hutchinson kept repeating, propped on one elbow, his hands on his stomach, his face ashen gray.

"Oh, Joshua," Rachel said. Tears ran down her cheeks as she pulled him, carefully away from the bed. "You shouldn't have done that.

"He . . . mighta shot . . . you, Miss Rachel," the big man managed from flat on his back while Rachel lifted his big head to her lap. "An' Mr. Ryan. He . . . mighta shot Mr. Ryan."

"Mr. Ryan?" Rachel managed, surprised that Joshua was concerned about Clint.

"Mr. Ryan, he . . . dragged me . . . outta that fire. He . . . coulda . . . died." The life fled from Joshua's eyes. They grew dim, and he closed them.

Rachel sobbed once, then collected herself and gently laid Joshua's head to the floor. Clint stood, the Root's hanging at his side.

Hutchinson still lay on the floor muttering. He raised fearful eyes to Clint. "Get me a doctor, Ryan," he pleaded. "I'm shot bad. I could die," he said, seemingly astounded at the notion.

Clint turned to head for the door, then heard Rachel's cold voice.

"There's no 'could' about it, Garth." The gunshot rang through the room. Clint jerked around to see the smoking Allen's in her hand, and Garth Hutchinson unmoving on his back with a small hole in his forehead, a trickle of blood crossing his cheek, his legs and arms splayed wide.

"No 'could' about it," Clint repeated, and sighed deeply.

"Drop that gun." The voice and running footsteps rang from down the hall. Clint whipped his head to see a swarm of deputies pouring down the narrow passage. He dropped the Root's and Rachel let the Allen's fall to the floor. Tears washed her cheeks, but she held her head high.

In seconds the deputies had surveyed the scene, clamped Clint in irons, and had them heading down the last flight of stairs to the lobby—where Clint spotted Toy and Boulders, also with irons on their wrists. Toy had one arm strapped across his chest with a belt, and his irons were oddly applied in front of him. His shoulder was caked with blood where Clint had torn the shirt away. Boulders, like Clint, had his irons on behind his back. Clint's side was soaked with blood from the groove cut by the ball.

The three Sydney Ducks who had been with Hutchinson lay in various stages of disarray on the lobby floor, and other deputies stood with Toy and Boulders in hand.

Boulders looked apologetically at Clint. "Toy and I would have been along soon as we finished down here, but the marshals had other ideas."

"Where've you been?" Clint asked, concerned.

"I been getting the smoke outta my gullet. The firemen dragged me outta the ol' New South Wales . . . but I got me a bunch a' those ol' Ducks first. Toy here did what ya told him and followed Hutchinson . . . followed ya'll here, then came an' fetched me. Hell, he whooped two of these ol' Ducks with one hand."

"You boys knock off the chitchat," one of the marshals ordered.

Rachel stood across the lobby, talking to another of the marshals, who repeatedly shook his head. Finally they walked over to where Clint and the others waited.

"I tried, Clint," she said, tears still tracking her cheeks.

"You're going to jail, Ryan," the deputy said.

"Maybe, but the man you should want is going nowhere . . . except maybe to the undertaker."

"You'll get your chance to tell it to the judge."

Clint sighed deeply, and the deputies led the three of them out.

"I'm sorry, Clint." Rachel's voice rang out behind them. "I'll get a lawyer for you."

"Stanhope," Clint called over his shoulder, then laughed wryly to himself. Stanhope would probably be a witness for the prosecution.

In less than half an hour, after being

treated and bandaged by one of the guards, the three of them were locked in separate cold dark cells, in separate parts of the jail.

It was two days before Stanhope made an appearance.

Clint's cell door rattled and he opened his eyes to see the lawyer standing there with a disgusted look on his face. Clint roused himself to set on the edge of his bunk.

"I hate these damned jails," Stanhope grumbled.

"They're getting to be my favorite places," Clint answered sarcastically.

"Must be, you seem to visit them often enough." Stanhope laughed quietly.

"Did Rachel come to you?"

"Yes . . . yes . . . damn fine-looking woman. One of the most refined and beautiful ladies I've ever had the, pleasure of meeting. I enjoyed dinner with her last evening.

Clint smiled to himself at the use of the word refined and thought of Rachel coldly shooting Hutchinson between the eyes. He hoped if Stanhope got close to the refined lady, he didn't cross her. But he said nothing to the lawyer about it, just as he had said nothing to the marshals. Rather, he changed the subject. "So are you going to defend Boulders, Toy, and me?"

"Nope," Stanhope said. Clint wasn't surprised. He lay back on his bunk. "You don't need defending," the lawyer added, and Clint quickly sat back up. "At least not for the original charges. Hutchinson had a money belt on him with a map in it."

Clint remembered that the man had not taken his shirt off when he got into the bed with Rachel, but again, didn't mention it.

"The undertaker found it," Stanhope continued. "Seems he hid the gold on Angel Island, right here in the bay. Adam's Express guards found all but a few pounds today."

"And the *Belle?*"

"At least a half-dozen men showed up at the courthouse in Sacramento in the days after you were arraigned. Every shot heard fired on the *Belle* was accounted for, and someone saw you *not* firing each and every one of them, or knew you were up in the pilothouse. Their sworn affidavits were delivered here to the marshal's office yesterday. Seems you've been cleared."

"Then what am I doing in this damned cockroach cage?"

"Seems there's a little matter of breaking out of the *La Grange*. Not to speak of suspicion of destroying half of the Barbary Coast."

"Big loss," Clint said.

"Some people think so. Anyway, Don Carlos Vega has gone all your bails; the court took his word as a man of property. And of course, I took twenty cords of wood for handling the matter. I'll have firewood for the next five years. It's better than chickens or goats." Stanhope stood aside and motioned Clint out the open door. Clint didn't hesitate, and moved into the hall.

"Speaking of Don Carlos," he said as they headed down the dingy hall to another barred door where a guard awaited. "What's happened with the Land Commission?"

"They've recommended leaving the title of Rio del Rio Ancho in the Vega name. It's not confirmed yet, but it's only a formality."

"Big of them," Clint said.

"I forgot during our last conversation . . . you owe me fifty dollars for that other matter. The Sharpentier agreement."

"What happened with that?"

Led by the guard, they reached another

barred door and passed out into a hallway. The bars were behind Clint now. He took a deep breath of free air, and it tasted sweet.

Stanhope laughed quietly. "I sent the agreement back after reviewing it, assuring them that you'd approved it and would sign it after it was first executed by Sharpentier. But his attorney in Monterey is a damned fool."

"I didn't ever approve it! But why's his attorney a fool?"

"As soon as he had Sharpentier sign it and they sent it back here for your signature, I took it before a judge, an old friend of mine, and he negated it. English law doesn't allow a witness to barter his testimony, Ryan. Not only that, but the judge forwarded it on to the marshal's office and asked them to follow up by seeing if the old warrant was still in effect, and if so, getting it recalled based on Sharpentier's signed statement—the very agreement he tried to coerce you with! All Sharpentier accomplished was the admission that you had no guilt in the matter of the *Savannah*. The marshal sent a letter, and request, to Washington to that end."

Clint sighed deeply, then his look hardened. "Good, then I can feel free to stomp

Sharpentier's ugly carcass all over the street the next time I cross his path!" They reached the end of the hall and walked out into the jail's main office.

Apolonia Vega beat Rachel DuBois to his side. Don Carlo Vega crossed the room slowly and extended his hand. Clint accepted it with a grateful smile and a "gracias." Toy and Boulders were close behind, and to Clint's amusement, repeated his Spanish, each with his own distinctive accent. Everyone present laughed.

"It looks as if you got it all done after all, El Lazo," Don Carlos said in his finest Castillian Spanish, shaking his head in wonder.

"Good, then I can get back to the Kaweah. At least I can as soon as I straighten out these other charges," Clint answered, also in Spanish.

"How about *your* wood yard?" Don Carlos asked, as always, ready to honor his word.

"With the *Belle* gone—" Clint started to say, but was interrupted.

Boulders, tiring of the language he didn't understand, stepped up along side Clint. "What are we gonna do, sit around here til they lock us back up?"

"Don Carlos is suggesting I get to work in the wood business."

"Hell, boy, there's a million ol' boats out there needin' wood." Boulders laughed and poked Clint in the ribs. Clint winced, for his side was a long way from healed.

"You poke me again, and we'll continue that—" he eyed the women and cleaned up his speech, "that elbows thing."

"Anytime, pilgrim," Boulders said, and guffawed.

"He is right, Clint, about the other boats," Apolonia said in English. Hope that he would stay shone in her lovely dark eyes.

Clint pondered for a moment, then returned his attention to the Don and his speech to Spanish. "How about this, Don Carlos? Toy Chang and Bob Blanchard here can partner up with me in the wood yard." He turned to the two door-filling big men and switched to English again. "The wood yard. You two don't have nothing else to do. A three way split—only I'm heading back to the Kaweah." Toy would finally get his fair share. Then Clint looked to Apolonia, who had a hurt look creeping across her pretty face. "But I'll be back soon. As soon as I make sure everything is going good at the ranch."

"That sounds fine to me," Boulders said, clapping Toy on the back hard enough to knock the wind from most men. Toy clapped him back, sending him forward a couple of steps. Boulders regained his balance, guffawed, then winked at Clint. "Fine with me, in fact fine as the fuzz on a new chick." Boulders repeated, then eyed Toy, who merely nodded his big head.

"Let's go somewhere to have a drink and seal the bargain," Clint said. He offered a smile and his arm to Apolonia while Stanhope did the same to Rachel. Don Carlos glanced from speaker to speaker, not understanding the language, but clearly understanding the smiles that passed between them.

Apolonia whispered to him, and he grinned in satisfaction.

Clint paused at the outside door and turned back to eye the jail. "Even a shot of bad whiskey tastes better than jail."

"I don't drink bad whiskey," Stanhope said, glaring down his nose at Clint. "Nor does Miss DuBois, and you're buying, my fine free friend. In fact, I've got fifty dollar's worth of drinks coming from you. Don't we, Rachel, dear?"

"Whatever you say, Clifford," Rachel smiled sweetly.

Clint wondered about Stanhope's reference to "friend," but followed willingly as the lawyer led the way down the boardwalk, happy that the "free" part was correct, and that he was with some who he could truly call *amigos*.